BOY WITH A PROBLEM

Short Stories

CHRIS BENJAMIN

POTTERSFIELD PRESS

Lawrencetown Beach, Nova Scotia, Canada

Library and Archives Canada Cataloguing in Publication

Title: Boy with a problem / Chris Benjamin.
Names: Benjamin, Chris, 1975- author.
Description: Short stories.
Identifiers: Canadiana (print) 20200278622 | Canadiana (ebook) 20200278630 | ISBN 9781989725276 (softcover) | ISBN 9781989725283 (EPUB)
Classification: LCC PS8603.E5578 B69 2020 | DDC C813/.6—dc23

Front cover credit: Dreamstime 172968068.jpg, © Jasonlee3071

Cover design: Gail LeBlanc

Pottersfield Press gratefully acknowledges the financial support of the Government of Canada for our publishing activities. We also acknowledge the support of the Canada Council for the Arts and the Province of Nova Scotia which has assisted us to develop and promote our creative industries for the benefit of all Nova Scotians.

Pottersfield Press
248 Leslie Road
East Lawrencetown, Nova Scotia, Canada, B2Z 1T4
Website: www.PottersfieldPress.com
To order, phone 1-800-NIMBUS9 (1-800-646-2879) www.nimbus.ns.ca

Printed in Canada

Pottersfield Press is committed to preserving the environment and the appropriate harvesting of trees and has printed this book on Forest Stewardship Council® certified paper.

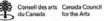   

To Miia; always to Miia

CONTENTS

BOY WITH A PROBLEM

During the year following the accident, the year he turns fourteen and moves from a tiny Nova Scotia village into the comparatively large capital city, Dan's favourite place becomes Aunt Chelsea's kitchen. He often sits at her round laminate kitchen table and listens to talk radio. The deep-voiced shock jocks make him laugh. They're verbal bullies – he can barely tell their voices apart – and he's a safe bystander, unseen and unheard, too young and unknown to be their prey. On a hot summer day when the sun through the window makes him sweat, they go on about drugs in the North.

"Here's a story from today's *Chronicle Herald*," one of them says. "Says half of all teenagers up in Frobisher Bay are addicted to alcohol, gas, or glue."

"What are the other half addicted to?" the other jock says.

Dan can tell by the jock's tone that it's a witticism. He obligingly laughs. Aunt Chelsea whips her head around and shoots him a look. But her shoulders stay square to the counter. She's working on her latest batch of sweets. "This'll cheer you up," she says, every day it seems, handing him a heaping plate of hot cookies or a steaming piece of pie.

"Dan," she says now. "That's not funny."

"Yes, Aunt Chelsea."

"I told you to drop it with the aunt stuff. No titles in this house."

"Seriously," the first jock is saying. "And if half of them aren't hooked yet, why aren't they doing something to stop the other half?"

"Here's what ticks me off," the second jock says.

Aunt Chelsea and Dan stare at the radio as if it's a charismatic guest in their home.

"These so-called experts, these social-policy wonks, are so fond of whining about *systemic* this and *systemic* that. Never is there any accountability on the part of the individual. What I'm saying is" – here the jock pauses dramatically – "Where does the buck stop, y'know? I'm sure the socialist media will blame the system ... or the white man. But hey, are we the ones drinking Frobisher Bay's babies to death?"

Dan looks away from the radio to Aunt Chelsea. She's stopped mixing whatever's in her bowl and stands still as a photo, except her mouth is opening and closing, like in a silent film. He notices for the first time she has the phone held to her ear. Aunt Chelsea still has her old rotary phone but it has a long chord.

"I'll hold," she says.

She shuts off the radio and turns to Dan. "Go listen to this in your room."

He runs up the stairs and flips on his boom box.

"Anyway, moving on," jock one says, "the city is facing yet another shortfall thanks to the big spenders at City Hall."

"Wait a minute," jock two says, "before we get into that I'm told we have a Chelsea MacDougall on the line from Halifax, and uh, she wants to talk about this Frobisher Bay situation."

"Holy shit, Aunt Chelsea," Dan whispers.

"Uh, yes, Mrs. MacDougall, go ahead. What do you know about it?" jock one asks.

"It's Ms. MacDougall," Aunt Chelsea's voice says through the radio. "And I don't know anything about it. I've never been there. Have you?"

There are a few seconds of dead air. "Well no, Ms. MacDougall, I haven't," jock one says. "But why would you call in about something you don't know anything about? I mean, we get a lot of, y'know, with all due respect, Ms. MacDougal, *morons* calling us with two-bit opinions ... and we're always happy to tear them a new one. But most of them at least have an opinion, Ms. MacDougall."

"You a little bored all alone at home today, Ms. MacDougall?" the other jock says.

"If you've never been to Frobisher Bay," Aunt Chelsea says, "why should we give a tiny shit about anything you have to say about it? Your opinions about the place – and mine – amount to absolutely nothing, you ... you pompous asses."

There's a loud click and another few seconds of dead air, followed by an outburst of deep-voiced laughter. "Well, sir, looks like we've been told by the bored spinster set," the first jock says.

"Dan! Supper," Aunt Chelsea hollers, her voice cracking.

Dan switches the radio off and runs back downstairs to the kitchen, where a tenor's bombastic voice fills the air. It's the first time Aunt Chelsea's ever changed the radio station on him since he moved in, right after the accident and his stupid, stubborn, hateful last words to his parents. What a clown he'd been.

"There's goulash on the table," Aunt Chelsea says.

He almost cries this time, having allowed himself to remember them. His dad used to make goulash for supper too. Instead of crying he smiles at Aunt Chelsea, sits down, and takes a bite. Dan hates goulash. But it doesn't matter like it used to.

Dan's problems start with the November writing thing, his English teacher's idea. "You're a good young writer," Mr. Lee tells him after class in late October. "Every November writers from all over the world try to write 50,000 words. Lots of young people do it. It's not competitive, just a chance to practise the art of writing. Wouldn't it be great to have written a novel at your age?"

His father is the novelist, and he doesn't want Dan to suffer the same fate. "Writers are the most miserable, sorry, insecure people on the planet," he says. But it's no surprise when he encourages the November novel writing idea. Dan knows the pattern well. His dad will be full of suggestions, euphoric at the chance to mentor his only child. Soon after, Dan will try out his father's proffered wisdom but he'll screw it up somehow. His father will immediately lose interest and grow distant again. Same as when Dan became a Boy Scout and his dad became a leader for exactly one camping trip. Same as when Dan took up the clarinet – his dad's old instrument – and his dad showed him how to care for the reeds, and when Dan left one attached to the mouthpiece inside the case his dad got mad and never went to any of his concerts. Dan is as powerless as his father to prevent the endless repetition of the pattern.

"I don't know where to start, Dad."

"Boy with a problem," his father says.

"Can you help though?"

"I am helping," he says, straddling a chair at the kitchen table. Dan has his laptop open to a blank document. "The basis of every great story is simple," his dad says. "You need a protagonist with a problem. Establish the problem on page one. Solve it by page three hundred. The rest is tension." He smells of aftershave and coffee and is wearing pajama bottoms and a white tank top, ready for bed. Dan's father is pretty much immune to caffeine.

"Why a boy then?" Dan asks.

"Write what you know."

Dan works on it for half the night.

There was a boy named David. And David loved Lucinda. Lucinda did not love him back.

No. He can't bear to write about unrequited love – too close to the bone.

Lucinda loved David as much as he loved her. The problem was, Lucinda was Catholic and David's parents were fundamentalist ... atheists.

"A satisfying twist to an old meme," he says to his dad in the morning, having rehearsed the line before bed.

His father hates the idea. "That won't carry you to page fifty. A cliché in a mirror is still a cliché."

"But you said all I needed was a boy with a problem."

"Different boy; different problem. Try again."

Dan exhales and slouches.

"Think about real boys you know. What are their problems? What are your problems?"

At lunch Dan walks one of the trails through the woods around his school, hoping for inspiration. Everyone else on the trail is smoking. At the end he finds a half-dozen smokers leaning against the property-line fence. "Hey," he says. They are grade twelves, three years older, gigantic.

"Hey," one of the girls says back. She doesn't look up. There are three girls and three boys. "What's wrong, buddy?" the girl asks, smoke rolling from her mouth. She's looking at him now, half smiling.

"Me?" he says. "Oh. Uh. Homework."

They all laugh.

"Can I ask you something?" he asks the girl.

"Shoot," she says.

"What are your big problems in life?"

They all laugh again. She doesn't answer at first. They take drags from their cigarettes.

"Seriously?" she says.

"Yeah."

"You a social worker?" one guy says. More chuckling.

"No. Kind of related to my homework. I won't use your names."

More laughter.

"You sound like a social worker," the guy says.

They all nod except the girl. "Well, buddy, if you really want to know ... my biggest problem is my asshole boyfriend can't stay away from Earla White!" She shoves the guy who spoke and the other four make a big show of laughing hysterically.

The guy shrugs. "My problem is I'm dating the second hottest girl in school with the first hottest temper."

She shoves him again, flicks his cigarette out of his hand, and storms away. "Come on, kid!" she shouts.

Dan looks at the guy with pity. "Sorry," he says.

"Come on!" the girl shouts.

"I think she means you, bud," the guy says.

"Oh," Dan says. He turns and runs to her.

"Men! That's my problem. Men," she says when he catches up.

"Really?"

"Really."

"Oh. But I need a guy's problem."

Without turning to face him she says, "A guy's problem? A guy's problem looks like this. He can't keep it in his pants; he gets two girls pregnant and tells them both to have abortions. And the nice, smart one agrees. But the slutty stupid bimbo says no, so the guy has to help raise a kid with a stupid slut he doesn't even like." She's crying as she speaks.

"Sorry," Dan says.

She turns around and hugs him. "You seem nice," she says. "Don't ever force a girl to make a choice like that, okay?"

He nods as she turns and runs away. He is unsure of her meaning, but feels excited by her story.

Dan's father hates the abortion storyline. "It'll come out preachy," he says. "Use the one about the atheists."

There it is; his father has dropped the project, and Dan with it. Dan shoves his laptop across the table. "You do it," he says.

"What's the point of that?"

What's the point of any of it? Dan's father would just be disappointed or worse, disinterested, whatever the outcome. How can anyone grow up in this godforsaken hellhole and be expected to come up with a novel anyway? Anyone with half a brain is mocked and teased and bullied or ignored. It was Dan's father who dragged him here and Dan's father who dismisses his best ideas. Dan sits there shaking, unable to articulate any of these things to his father. Instead he shouts the least intelligent thing he can think of: "Fuck you, Dad!"

His father winces when he hears Dan say "fuck." Dan can't stand that look of agony. He stands and goes to his room, locks the door behind him, and crawls into bed. A few minutes later his father pounds hard on his door, threatening to kick it down if he doesn't open it. Shocked as he appeared by Dan's use of the f-word, his father is using it liberally now. He's lost his temper like this before. Not often though, and usually at his wife.

Dan's mother intervenes with a gentle knock. "Dan?" she calls. "You got two options, pal. Apologize to your dad or we don't pay for your Christmas band trip. No Toronto."

And she starts a slow count to three. As if he's still a baby. They've been using the same trick all his life. Make him choose between what they want him to do and some unfathomably horrible alternative fate. You want the bullet to the temple or the knife to the throat? Choose.

He has to go to Toronto. He's been waiting all his life.

"Two," she counts.

He spits a one-word apology through the locked door. "Sorry!"

"Come out here and look in his eyes when you say it," she says, calm but firm.

He gets out of bed, walks slowly to the door, opens it, and looks directly at his father's feet. "Sorry," he mutters, and closes the door.

She knocks again. "Enough. Apologize with respect or lose the trip."

He manufactures just enough respect to calmly apologize, saying the words his mother needs to hear, like he always does. It doesn't make him or his father happy, but he gets to go to Toronto.

The perpetual avalanche of humans rushing through downtown Toronto makes him painfully anxious. He's so been looking forward to this trip, and rehearsing at Roy Thompson Hall with a professional conductor. But mostly it's the city he wanted: the size, the life. When their bus rolled through an eternity of superhighway he started to feel it pulsing, something super-electric, a billion megawatts burning at once. But cold. The sun is only visible by its reflection in the banks.

Following his classmates around to the sights has been awful. These backwater bozos have a better knack for navigating the anthill than he does. The pulse paralyzes him. And the sights: the Eaton Centre shopping spree; a live basketball game; a communications tower resembling a monolithic phallus. Everything turned up: too big, too loud, and too fast.

His parents. He can't stop thinking about them. How they hate Toronto, take every opportunity to delight in its failures, yet keep checking its concert and gallery listings. "Why can't we get art like that here? We have enough artists you'd think we'd merit one Modigliani show, just once!" Dan has never forgiven them for taking him away from the real city before he was old enough to archive its smells. And he can't stop thinking about them, how he cursed them to hell before he left. He's still angry, yet he knows he is at least partially responsible.

After they leave the CN Tower he falls behind the group, feeling woozy. He stands on Front Street in the cold, is nearly trampled by masses of strangers. He looks at his home number on the screen of his phone. He imagines his father's hello, and what he should say. "Sorry, Dad. I know you were trying to help." But he puts the phone back in his pocket.

She's a peculiar creature, this Halifax aunt. He'd met her a few times before the accident and she always seemed like a person who could be busier than anyone else and have less to show for it. She's forever cleaning a filthy house, working on an incomplete masterpiece, complaining about a world that's lost its way.

That's the most entertaining part: her arguments with the news. As far as he knows, she's only actually called in to one of these shows the one time, when she told off the shock jocks. Mostly she's content talking to Dan or to herself, chastising the politicians of all partisanships, the reporters for their lack of affiliation, and occasionally the current affairs hosts for their faux objectivity. "Who picked these two extremists? What a bunch of ugly nothing. There's no nuance when a cat fights a dog."

Sometimes she apes a politician, the mayor being her favourite. Her impression of the mayor is a cross between a tongue-tied silver-spoon conservative Quimby and Elmer Fudd. "Er uh, ba-daa ba-daa, I uh, I stick to what I said before about not saying the thing that, uh, ahh, is being said that I said." She makes him laugh with that. She's the first to make him laugh after the car accident.

He came home early, alone on an airplane, no Roy Thompson Hall rehearsal with a real conductor. He went straight to Aunt Chelsea's, practically a stranger, but he came to her weary and she put him to work assembling an old cot she bought at the Army & Navy. "The deals you get there – and good stuff too. I got all my kitchen knives there. I don't know why people buy all this new made-in-China stuff from Walmart. A million square feet of hell that is. Look, Dan. Still in the box. Help me put it together."

And it hasn't stopped – her tongue, the work. Constant as the radio playing in the background.

"How am I supposed to work on my writing if I have to sweep the floors every night?" he complains.

"I thought you wanted to be a photographer."

"I'm not good with machines," he says.

She laughs. "So much like your father. And our dad and him used to *fight*, oh my."

"What about?"

"Everything. Politics. Chores. Art. By the time he was eighteen your dad couldn't wait to flee. Halifax wasn't even big enough anymore, or far enough away. Keep in mind your grandfather didn't see a car till he was ten years old. Anyway, you know the rest."

"Tell me anyway."

She whacks her nose side to side with her index knuckle, a habit he can't figure out if it's nervous or excess energy. "Anyway. The irony is if not for all those farm chores I don't think your dad would have finished his novel."

"He wrote what he knew, and he knew farming because of Grandpa."

"The chores taught your dad discipline. He would always say, 'A novel's a marathon.'"

"How come he never wrote another one?"

"What's this story here, Dan? Turn up the radio now." She shuffles around him and does it herself. "Twinning the highway. What a waste of millions. And still no abortion clinic in rural Nova Scotia for God's sake."

It's ten months since the accident. Ten months of sweeping and washing and gardening and raking a ramshackle house that never looks clean. And finally he cries. She's on him with the speed of an insect but with hugs and kisses for his hair. "Dan, we should make some cookies," she says.

"Maybe if the roads were better they wouldn't have died," he says, scarcely a whisper.

"Oh, Dan." She hugs him, head to chest. She doesn't list them but he can hear her counterarguments, the big-picture reasons why the road shouldn't be widened, all that money to maybe, maybe not, save a few lives. He's heard the speech on other issues: spraying pesticides, building skyscrapers. His parents would agree with her.

"I should write a letter," he says.

"If you think it'll help."

"To the radio station."

"Sure."

"And I should finish my novel."

"You have a novel?"

"Sure," he says. "It's about abortion."

"Your father would be so goddamned proud."

MULCH GLUE

Start with a newspaper. Twitter's okay, but scattered. Nothing enrages like the focus of a newspaper, a deep dive into one corporation's officially approved perspective. Its particular valuations of each life, each species. I may be a GenZ gal, but I'm not in a bubble. Mr. Trumann turned out to be full of shitake when he said I was. He was probably just freaked because I called out how fake his Vision Board activity was.

"You were supposed to come up with your vision of the future of this town." Staring from behind his desk at my blank board, he had a fist over his heart and a hand over the fist, like he was trying to pull the knife out. *Et tu*, teacher's pet?

"Exactly. This town has no future."

My classmates tittered like nothing mattered so what but they didn't get it. They don't see the writing on the water. It's easy to get them crying about how much our parents and grandparents have fricked up the world. Yet they'd all pasted images of big-city skyscrapers on their Vision Boards. As if all the Bildebergers were at that moment scouring what remained of the planet for just-the-right pulp town to reclaim. Even Maisy Best, who started the Eco-Guardian Club, which had me as one of its five members, couldn't think past Earth Day garbage pickups and handing out Idle Free flyers at the Kiss 'N Ride. Her Vision Board was covered in glossy magazine cut-outs of waterfalls, whales underwater, and a rainforest.

I stood there with my blank Vision Board held high.

I wanted to shout, "This is our future, don't you see?" but I said nothing, just like the other kids said nothing to their parents about how the mill they worked at was destroying the air we breathed and the water we couldn't drink. Mr. Trumann, educator of future visionaries, told me I needed to look outside my little bubble.

Well, the man is named for truthfulness, so I took him at his word. For weeks I've been trying to look outside my bubble. Faithfully reading the local newspaper.

Here's what I see:

They're digging up a graveyard full of Native American veterans' bones to put up a wall to keep out desperate Mexicans.

It's the second week of hurricane season, and the second hurricane is already on its way. Probably because the North Atlantic was warm enough to swim in back in July, comfortably, floating like you were in the Caribbean Sea, sipping rum punch, if you were old enough, which in the Caribbean maybe you were.

Poverty.

Billionaires.

Poor people.

Not-for-profits dropping cash on billboards begging government to clean up messes made by megacorporations, like it promised to but probably never intended to.

Woman killed here, woman killed there, backwater to capital, next door and far away. Killed by stalkers, killed by shattered men vacuumed of hope and infused with rage in Afghanistan. Killed by billionaires. Killed by poverty.

Fascists attack other fascists' oil, still other fascists blame a fourth set of fascists, who throw their hands in the air and scream out, "Maximum Lies!"

My dad drives all over town in his twentieth-century Plymouth looking for cheaper gas. He says even if he wastes a little gas, he saves money if he finds the right price. I tell him they can always print more money but there's only so much gas in the ground and only so much CO_2 the climate can stand. He says *money don't grow on trees.*

My therapist tells me this is not my fault. She says everybody's got the same condition now, whether they know it or not, but we fortunate ones can at least afford therapy. None of us are happy people.

There are other ways I've tried busting out of my bubble. I read all Mom's Thoreau books. I've spent hours and nights cracked out on Internet chat rooms talking politics. There are boards from all over the political spectrum. Communist boards. Truther boards. Alberta Separatist boards. Stop Immigrants from Stealing Jobs boards. You might think all those different ideas would shatter a kid's brainstem. I figure everyone's coming to the same place, no matter their sources. That place we're all gathering, it's filthy.

I don't have to go anywhere to see the filth. I don't need a screen or a printed page. I just look out my window. The incoming tide looks like infectious mushroom caps invading the rocks of Vessel Cove. Dad claims that when he closes his eyes, he can still feel his body tighten in the air, as if he's just launched himself from the pier and is bracing for impact with the water, for the icy relief of the Atlantic on an eternal August day. A scene from long before the Plymouth. He remembers swimming with the fishes when it was a literal thing living people did, eyes open and stinging against the saline, some of those fishes longer than him.

Old man tales, Mom calls Dad's rambling. It is hard to imagine Dad all wild and free. But Mom says she fell in love the moment she saw Dad's ripped, tanned arms hauling in a giant cod on the line, into Grandpa's boat. My Grandpa had a motherfricking sailboat. He went all up and down the coast on it, singing sailor songs probably. "I wish I was a fisherman." This was after he retired from the mill and before he died of lung cancer, when I was seven.

It's hard to picture, when I watch the brown foamy waves roll in, swarmed by ropey green insects, and when I smell the chemical soup they're lapping up. I swear those bugs are immunizing themselves in preparation for our extinction, preparing to zip into our role as world overlords. Those chems emit a sweet smell; it's the smell of home, and it's disgusting. Trillions of litres of Eastern Mulch swill have done that to the Cove, even if the megacorporation does conform to federal emissions standards and has passed dozens of low-grade impact assessments; human science is corrupt like that. We don't drink the tap water. We leave it to fuel the green bugs.

I like those Thoreau books though. They're the cleanest thoughts I've seen, especially that stuff about civil disobedience. If you're looking for a life to model yours after, you could do worse than Thoreau. If you're a man. If you've got some money stashed away. And if you can find a patch of forest that the megacorporations haven't got to yet. But I like reading it. It's like this bag of nineteenth-century bones is speaking to me, like I am the powder monkey marching in admirable order, straight into the megacorporation's sludge, and it fires me the frick up. The machine must fall? You bet.

But my parents trip over this stuff. I can't even talk to my mom about her own books. I tell her I'm amped up about making my life a counter-friction to Eastern Mulch and she sits me down for a "chat," which means it's time for a lecture on this theoretically new concept called eco-anxiety.

"And this is how the world doesn't change," I say.

"Excuse me, I change the world every day, one child at a time."

This is what Mom thinks primary school teachers do. "And yet when this child wants to do something about the world, you crush her spirit."

"I want your spirit to soar, Bree. Which is why you should enjoy being a child. We don't want you to get hurt."

"But I am hurting."

Mom asks for time to think on it. After school she texts me links to a video about activist burnout, some stuff on the need for self-care, and a story about a guy who got arrested when he was a teenager for locking himself to a bridge. Later he wasn't allowed to go to med school in the U.S. He says he could have made a real difference as a doctor. As if they don't have med schools outside the U.S.

Let's call Thoreau my flint. My match was a chat board where stay-at-home nerds talked Extinction Rebellion. I've tried talking with some of the kids at school about this stuff but most of them have parents who work at the mill. I thought Soph, whose family immigrated from a war zone, might understand even though she isn't a member of the Eco-Guardian Club, but she said "peace is built on forgiveness." I'm still not sure what she means.

On the *Action Now!* chat board we talk about people who glue themselves to buildings or trains. It drives the cops crazy because if they want to haul your ass away first they have to rip your skin off. Tearing off an old lady's ass skin makes for bad press. The problem is Eastern Mulch's headquarters is in China, in a city I won't offend by trying to pronounce. Their only property here is the mill, which is on top of a little hill and looks like some kind of weird robot made with different Lego sets collected over the years, parts all mixed up in one bucket. It's a brick rectangle with pipes sticking out, some vertical, some horizontal, all of them billowing white-grey-black chemical fluff.

I've lived here all my fifteen years, yet I never went up that little hill, into the belly of the robot. Unlike most of the bullies at my school, I'm not a mill rat; my parents don't work there. Dad's a librarian and Mom's a teacher. I never had any cause to be there.

After school on Friday I walk up Eastern Connector, past Mister Pizza and the Hortons toward the highway, and stick my thumb out. A youngish woman with round black glasses picks me up almost right away. From the orange safety vest over her blue dress shirt I know where she's headed. When I tell her my dad works at the mill she wants to know who he is, and I say my daddy's name is Muhammed. She looks at me all weird so I tell her I'm adopted. I should have said Dad converted after 9/11, but she lets it go without demanding I open my backpack, without discovering my crazy glue, which is what I assume to be the cheap shit. The brand name is "Mulch," an irresistible coincidence. I was all psyched up by the hilarious Gorilla Glue commercials but this was what Mom had stashed in our junk drawer. This mill woman looks all suspicious again when she stops the car and I ask where the robot's front door is. I follow her up the walk and stop when I see the door, a sheen of glass in the middle of all the brick and aluminum. I say my dad's meeting me here and thank her for the lift. When she's gone I slip off my Nikes so I'm barefoot.

How the frick am I going to get myself glued to this door? I'd briefly imagined myself doing this naked, "MY BODY HANDS OFF!" spray painted over my chest, but the last thing I needed was a bunch of dudes streaming out the front door perving on my exposed skin. The workers all wear blue jeans and flannel. Where are the suits? I want to chicken out but I already left a manifesto in three different chat rooms and sent a press release to the local paper and the CBC. I signed it Zelda McGee.

I wait for a lull in foot traffic, occasionally getting jostled by denim dudes going in or out. One stares at me for a few seconds and I can't tell if he's got a foot fetish or is just curious about my bare feet. When there's finally no one around, I slather the glue on four spots on the outside of the door, measuring the distance with my reach, from feet to hands, spread-eagled, the foot spots a couple inches off the ground. It helps that I'm short and skinny. I close my eyes, breathe deep, run, and hurl myself at the spot, but I don't hit the door evenly so I bounce off. The door shakes with the impact.

I catch my breath and push my right foot against its glue spot, roll into it a bit. My foot slips right through the glue, slapping the pavement hard enough to hurt. The left foot does the same shitty thing from its glue spot. I push my right palm against one of the higher spots, cursing the cheap glue and expecting the same result I got with my feet, but my palm sticks; my hand and the glass have merged. I get the same result with my left palm. I'm stuck to the door, face pressed against the glass so that I'm staring into the lobby, which is bigger than I expected, with a wide wooden arched stanchion dominating its centre, elevators on either side of it. I'm tiptoeing to reach my hand spots. I lean in and let myself hang slightly but it's a torture session, straining the skin of my palms, so I tip-toe again, taking the weight off my hands.

A grey-eyed older man, who resembles a rat with superfluous facial hair and an overbite, gives my heart a jolt and I let out a squeak. He came out of nowhere. He approaches the door from inside the building, wanting to exit. I half smile like a stunned nub, stretched against the glass, him pointing to the handle and mouthing, then shouting so I can hear. "Can I come out?" Like I'm his boss. And I am. My smile grows and now it's all greased up, yeah, motherfricker, I am your boss. He shrugs, looking antsy for an answer and I realize this is my moment so I start my chant.

"No! More! Eastern Mulch! Wrong! Side! Of the gulch!"

The guy looks around for the hidden camera, smiling awkwardly like it's a birthday prank, but after a few incantations he gets the point. He shrugs at me, wondering what he should do next, so I pause my chant and yell directly at him.

"Go tell your bosses."

He shrugs again, looks over his shoulder, then his other one, and pushes the door. I'm jolted backwards, my feet dragging on the pavement, the tips of my toes against the bottom of the door, leaving bloodspots, and I'm screaming at this fricking mill rat.

"Careful with my feet – this is a protest, you fat lumberjack."

"Good luck, kid. Nice chant." He says this while holding the door open for another mill rat, who thanks him and walks through without looking at me.

"You try rhyming mulch," I say.

Lumberjack lets go and I lift my feet for the ride back into the door's closed position. My palms stretch with my weight, which feels like being attacked by a billion flesh-eating ants, like I have to suck my teeth with all my strength to prevent myself from screeching, only to see two more guys coming from inside. They push right through, ignoring me as I swing forward again and get another view of the lobby.

"Don't you see me here?" I'm craning my neck so I don't have to shout directly into the glass. "It's a protest."

"For higher wages?" says a bald-headed dude with a white goatee. I have to pivot my head to the left and look way over my shoulder to see him. He and his companion have joined the first guy who exited to make a party of three workers. "Your dad work here?"

"This is for the Cove."

The three of them laugh and head to their cars.

I look back into the lobby to see the elevator doors open. Out pours a pack of workers. They come toward me in a mass, round men in hoodies, jeans, yellow and orange safety vests, holding their hard hats, backpacks slung over their shoulders – they look like puffed-out wrinkled versions of the boys at school – smiling and cracking their end-of-shift jokes, competing to see who can laugh loudest. Before they reach me I feel myself yanked backwards, the world swinging circumferentially sideways until I see who pulled me: a less dusty version of the men on their way out, an old dude heading in for the late shift, a bulbous pouch under his chin. With a free hand he pulls his glasses farther down his nose to peer over them. He doesn't speak, just gazes questioningly as the safety-vested crowd streaming from the building surrounds us. They all have the same confused expression, similar to my mom's. Like they're trying to decide whether to give me a timeout or a hug.

"Who are you?" someone says.

I try to start up my chant again but my tongue trips. The words suck anyway. I shout the only thing I can think of. "This is for the Cove! This is for the Earth!"

So many eyes roll I think they're emitting thunder but I realize that's actually the sound of their boots walking away. They are pushing past me, swinging me back and forth as the pain in my hands stabs my brain, so I can think of nothing but the weight of my body tearing skin from my hands micrometre by micrometre. I try to collect myself, breathe baby breathe, but my face is pressed against the glass. I remind myself to bend my legs at the knees as the workers brush past me, to save my feet. But it hurts my hands more and I'm not sure which is worse. I lift my head away from the glass and open my mouth to scream. I let loose my defiant chant, shout it boldly because frick them all if they can't see what their work is doing to the world.

One guy with a voice like George Ezra's grandpa stops to talk, standing behind me with a leathery hand on my shoulder. There's something familiar in his touch, a warmth that makes it easier to breathe. He doesn't ask what I'm doing or why, doesn't seem to wonder about global clusterfricking, which is what I call climate chaos, or about my anger or fear or anxiety or any of the reasons I'm doing this. About my tanned father swimming and fishing. But he does ask me, simply, "Are you okay, sweetheart?" He offers to call 911 for help.

I beg him not to and hate myself for saying please.

"What about your parents, dear? Does your father work here? I can go get him for you."

I shake my head as best I can in my predicament.

"Ah, of course." He says it as if my father's absence at

the mill explains everything, as if I wouldn't be here if I relied on Eastern Mulch's brown foamy lucre. I hate most of all that he might be right. I didn't glue myself to the library when they had a talk by the author of a book called *Charm Her Pants Off*.

A few minutes after George Ezra's grandpa goes away, and just as the mill is settling into its late shift, two cop cars paint the scene red and fill the air with siren wails. Four uniforms come at me, guns aligned with their pants stripes, one of them I think was my reading buddy in elementary school and the rest are grumpy old men, and I want to take a cheese grater to George Ezra's grandpa for ratting me out, hate myself for feeling that maybe he did it because he was worried about me. The four of them stand around, waving onlookers away, asking each other questions. One of the white-hairs tugs at my arm and I regret not using the body paint. I tell him to frick off, it hurts.

"Glue?" he asks, but I'm using my Miranda as seen on *Law & Order: Special Victims Unit*. The Cove is the special victim.

It's hard to converse with my back to them and my face against the glass, stretched out on tippy toes. Nothing about this is comfortable, and it gets worse when the four of them grab me, two at each shoulder, and start pulling. I scream Shakespearean insults from Dad's bathroom reader so hard my throat rips. "Away, you stock-fish!"

They're too busy instructing each other on proper pulling techniques to abide my pain, but someone takes the time to make a suggestion. "Maybe try acetone?" a mystery voice says.

At first I think it's Book Buddy. The voice mellifluous and young. But then I notice Book Buddy is busy trying to wedge himself between me and the door. He's seeing if he can push harder than he pulls. My eyes boil looking into his and I hope he can feel me hating him for his gross personal-space invasion with his oval body and pointy hands, and his musky body spray. So it's definitely not him who made the suggestion.

But he eventually disentangles himself from me and joins the other cops as they interrogate the guy who suggested acetone, like who the frick is he and what's he know about glue and who authorized him to talk anyways? When the man identifies himself as a journalist from the local paper I thank the whole Universe, someone got my press release and cared enough to come, a lone soldier of investigation and knowledge sharing. I can hear all this in his earnest voice. It is an ode to grounded rationality. Surely he's on a truth kick, binging on facts like a junkie out of rehab, seeking out objectivity like an elixir inside the Holy Grail.

The cops tell him to frick off. They make a swift turn and they're right back at it, grabbing and yanking harder, rocking me back and forth like a car in a snowbank, like they want to tear me to pieces, and I literally bite down on my tongue to hold back a scream because I won't give these frickers the satisfaction. I hate them for making me want to cry, for making me think Mom was right, for making me wish we had cops like those nice British Bobbies who didn't want to hurt the old ladies who tried this same stunt over in England. They make my hands feel like the chalk we dissolved in vinegar in chemistry class. The superglue has made me and this glass building one object, and they need to undo the melding.

The reporter shouts the word "acetone" like an irate mantra until he finally decides to insert himself into the story, diving into the fray with his palms together to split the cops up and get to me. Will his story wax poetic on the beauty of my Mulch Glue?

I gasp as I feel my body move back, howl when my hands are loosed from the door, and howl more when I look to see blood coming from my palms as the cops drag me. My toes are bleeding too from all the scraping on the ground. I don't have Jesus' stoicism, am more animalistic. I lick the blood away from my palms and it tastes like glue. "Throw me in the woods," I say, but we all know there are no woods left around here.

From the corner of my eye I see a boomer in jeans and a plaid shirt, arms folded and shaking his head like Mom does when she thinks I'm too young to understand something. From his hands I know it's George Ezra's grandpa. I hear his deep, cracked voice in my head, accusing me, "Don't you know how lucky you are?"

Or maybe it's my own grandpa's voice.

What George Ezra's grandpa actually says is quite different. He calls out the name of one of the older cops, and when he has his attention he says, "She's not a bad kid."

I notice, as they help me up into the back of it, that a police van has arrived. The reporter is already in there, arrested for having interfered with the police as they interfered with my protest. He looks right at me, his face a picture of curiosity and regret. I don't think he planned on being arrested today, poor guy. Maybe it was him who was my reading buddy in elementary school. I had such a crush on that kid, with his long black hair and inquisitive blue eyes, a few mysterious grades ahead of me in life. Everyone looks familiar in this town but I'm not good with faces or names. It doesn't matter. This guy broke the fourth wall for me, stepped out of his narrative. He was moved by my anguish. There's hope. Now I can tell him about Thoreau, in case he isn't familiar. Although I suppose he'll miss his deadline.

"You got my press release."

"I worried it might be a joke. Why would a nice kid like you do something like this all by yourself?"

Frick. It's my mom all over again. "Why's every adult outside the cops want to protect me from harm but doesn't give a half-shit what's happening to the Cove?"

"Okay."

"I bet you know people who work here."

"Who doesn't?"

I go back to licking at my hands, then give up and hold them against my pants, which aren't super absorbent but the

bleeding isn't really all that bad. We hit a bump and the reporter and I both pop up from our respective benches and land
again on our butts.

He smiles like he enjoys the adventure. "Well, as long as
we're here, why don't you tell me more about yourself then,
Zelda?"

By the way I smile he sees right away that Zelda, the war-
rior name I used for my press release, is not what I'm really
called.

"It's Bree."

"Bree," he says. "Well, you got me here. Care to tell me
about yourself? Do your parents work at the mill? Do they
know what you're up to? Are they supportive?"

I sit there, looking into his blue eyes, which are not as glit-
tering and far-minded as my old book buddy's were, thinking
of where to begin. I really don't want to talk about myself, even
though my mind goes back to my dad, stretched out above the
water, the moment before impact, his body young and strong
and tensed, the elation of it. If I talk about that, people won't
get it. They won't see what it's got to do with gluing myself
to the mill. And if I talk badly about the mill they'll think I'm
against the workers. I wait a long time before speaking, long
enough to get irritated by the sound of the reporter's Oxfords
tapping the floor of the van, and the slight echo through our
little cavern.

OPERATION NIBLET

Zoëy taught Gerry – who was always in love with animals and every year painted several landscapes featuring majestic moose in wide-open fields – about how people think animals are property but they're not; they're sentient and have a right to live and enjoy smelling and tasting and seeing beauty. Eating them was wrong, and he wouldn't do it anymore.

Terry and Sue, their other roommates, were also vegans. They were much more radical than Zoëy. They had each served time. Terry was convicted of assaulting a security guard and Sue snatched a wad of cash off an inattentive bank teller and burned it, setting off the fire sprinklers. Gerry loved their stories of defiance and lockup, like Bonnie and Clyde if they'd survived all those bullets from the posse. Zoëy was captivated by their ideas and questioned them like a reporter seeking the perfect sound bite.

Maybe it was the weed, the fact that Gerry smoked and they didn't, but when they all sat together on the front porch he was often stunned into silence by the things Terry and Sue said. Their words seemed hazy and unfathomable but he loved listening anyway. He loved it when they called people pussies – he hadn't expected that from lesbians.

But he was also glad they weren't night owls like him and Zoëy. When Sue stood and held her hands out to help Terry up, and led her by the hand, inside to their shared room, it was the happiest moment of Gerry's daily routine. It was when he got Zoëy alone and they could talk about her more nuanced ideas.

At such a time he told Zoëy about his mother, specifically about his experience witnessing the moose the day she left him with a bullshit story, how the majestic animal gave him strength to carry on despite the loss, how he had had many dreams of moose since, of being a half-moose half-man unsuccessfully harvesting wild rice with hooves, and of his previous life as a (possibly female) member of the Moose Clan of the Mamaceqtaw people of what is now called Wisconsin.

As he spoke he tried to read her eyes but as usual her Mona Lisa's visage revealed nothing of whatever she might be feeling. Inside she could have been laughing or crying or wondering how she came to be alone with this maniac. When he finished his story he fought, for the two hundredth time, the impulse to lean in and kiss her, and he wondered why he fought the impulse when his victory over it gave him only regret. Several minutes passed in the quiet of the city night. Gerry searched the sky and saw a blurred light that might have been a bright star or a muted streetlight on a distant hill.

"It's a great metaphor for civilization," Zoëy said finally. "How it's taken ownership over everything and you could never accept that. Could you, Gerry? So, your very wildness prevents you from living in any kind of traditional way." She pulled out a baggie of weed from her jeans. "Speaking of which, do you know about the animal testing going on at Dal?"

He shook his head.

"It's totally insane. They drill holes into the brains and eyes of kittens, puppies, rabbits, and mice while they're still alive, just to install things – poisons, monitors. When the experiment is done they kill them."

"Why would they do that?" Gerry said, horrified.

"Trying to cure blindness, stuff like that. They kill them by the millions in labs all over the world."

"Because they think they're our property," Gerry said.

"What would your Mamaceqtaw people think of that, Gerry?"

He shrugged and accepted the joint from her. "I think maybe the Moose Clan would think it's our job to fight back."

"That's what Terry said when I told her about it. That we have to fight back."

Gerry took a toke. He told Zoëy about the time he tried to free a local drug dealer's pit-bull puppies, when he was nine years old. He expected her to laugh but there was no reason to. She was a serious person. He appreciated that about her because it made him realize he'd played the clown too many times in his life.

"I wish I'd known you then," she said.

He smiled, feeling like there may not come a better time to kiss her. But he was always uncertain of her meaning. Did she wish she'd known him then because they were soulmates? Maybe because he was so badass back then but he had gone soft. Maybe she wished she'd known him then and taught him these things before he got so suburbanized.

"Maybe that's what we should do at the vivisection lab," she said, smiling then in earnest, showing her slightly crooked teeth on the bottom, and the more perfect ones on top, overbiting slightly, as if embarrassed by what was happening underneath them. If he kissed her would that be a problem or would the fullness of her lips cushion the blow?

"The mother dog left me with a limp for weeks. I'm lucky I didn't get rabies."

"These are bunny rabbits and mice, Gerry," she said. "And a few puppies. No angry mamma dogs."

He knew he'd do it if she were serious, that he'd do anything she asked really. He wished he could make them kids again so she could know him at that age, whatever her reasoning.

"How do we get in?" he said.

Terry and Sue proved invaluable in what they called Operation Niblet, after the kind of wound Gerry might sustain should a bunny rabbit react as the drug dealer's dog had done in his last animal heist. They came up with an elaborate plan to break into the lab and release as many mice and rabbits as they could into Point Pleasant Park, take a few kittens and puppies to give friends as pets. They spent several days scoping the place, walking around it from a comfortable distance and then sneaking in with help from a sympathetic friend of a friend who did janitorial shift work there. They got floor plans from the university archives and they mapped out an escape route.

They borrowed a friend's dark green minivan and took out the backseat to make room for the cages. Terry would drive. Sue and Zoëy would be the lookouts. The custodian they knew would help them get in without tripping alarms. And Gerry got the glory job. "You're skinny and strong and I bet you can run fast," Terry said. "The cages are only locked with padlocks, so you can bust them open with a hammer and chisel."

Gerry had a mild adrenaline rush thinking about it. He'd agreed to participate in a criminal mission for the sake of a hippie girl. A hippie girl he happened to love. He'd gone insane. "Ever hear the expression 'herding cats'?" he said.

"You grab whatever you can carry, leave the rest running around the building, wreaking havoc. And smash the shit out of every computer you see, take any disks you find."

"What will that accomplish?"

"The PETA freaks haven't accomplished shit," Terry said. "All their sternly worded letters and listserv groups. Useless. They go right on torturing and killing. No animals are saved by that bullshit."

He didn't see how this would be any different, which made the risk he was taking all the more absurd. Zoëy. She was so hot she made him physically ill, and apparently mentally ill too. It made no sense, but he couldn't stop thinking it: if he could get through this thing unscathed, then he could kiss her.

The plan was simple: all Gerry had to do was go to a basement window at exactly 3:00 a.m., a window that was never used but would be unlocked by their inside person, who had also popped in earlier in the evening to turn off the alarm. The building was patrolled by campus security, but Terry reassured him it was vacant from 3:00 to 4:00. Gerry would go alone, dressed all in black with a balaclava because of the video surveillance, with the hammer and chisel hanging from his belt. The green minivan would be outside waiting the whole time.

He was two minutes late arriving, but that left plenty of time. He glanced around for the van but didn't see it. It would be there. He pulled the window open and crawled down, ducked under the ceiling pipes, and ran to the stairs on the far side of the room.

The stairs were sunk in darkness but he'd been told there were eight large steps. As he counted seven there was a deafening crash and he felt blood rush to his nose. He turned on his flashlight to look at a heavy metallic door. It had blood on it. His blood. They'd given him the wrong number of stairs. He'd been lured into this insanity by amateurs, gifted bullshitters clueless when it came to capers.

"Fuck," he whispered. Before it could dry, he wiped it off with the inside of one of his black gloves. The inside was white cotton. He spit and wiped, spit and wiped, wondered about DNA, and realized he was damned either way. The best he could do was clear up the visual evidence. He looked at his watch: 3:07. "Fuck."

He tried the door. Locked. "Fuck. For fuck's sake!" He kicked it and hurt his foot. There was no way in. He flashed his light down the stairs and descended, willing his muscles to experience each movement, ignoring his heart pounding at the back of his eyeballs. It took him several minutes to get back to the window, and he felt a surge of relief when it opened.

He had tried his best and there was nothing left to do, though his chest heaved for the failure to earn that kiss that stared him in the face each night, so clear from such distance.

Gerry pulled himself up onto the grass and looked again for the van. No sign of it. No matter. With no animals he could ditch the balaclava and bloodied gloves and walk home.

"Hold up a minute," a voice said.

Gerry glanced over his left shoulder and froze at the sight of a security guard ambling toward him. The guard froze at the sight of Gerry, in his all-black balaclava suit. He wished he could stroll to the guard and put his arm around him and point to the trees at some hidden camera. Ha ha, what a farce!

Instead, Gerry bolted, slipped on the wet grass, and lurched forward into a puddle. He got up and ran again, his feet squishing with each step. Gerry sprinted south and cut to a side street all the way to Point Pleasant Park. He scanned his surroundings for the van. He was afraid to look back, but he was pretty sure he'd lost his security friend. He collapsed under a tree and laughed so hard tears ran down his cheeks. Someday he'd give the boys back home a huge laugh with this story. For now, he wanted to see Zoëy.

Zoëy apologized a million times for not showing up. A cop had pulled them over on their way. They were so nervous about the slim possibility of that very occurrence that they were driving too far below the speed limit.

The cop, on seeing what looked like three dykes crawling along at 2:30 a.m., was suspicious. But they were dressed normally – for them – Terry and Sue with their multicoloured hair, khaki pants, and button-up shirts, and Zoëy with her dreads and hoodie and tight brown cords. The cop looked in the back of the van and found a couple dozen small animal cages.

"I'm a vet," Terry said.

"Get out, all of you," the cop said. He checked their

pockets and ran their licenses, but they weren't wanted for anything anymore and there was no evidence of any wrongdoing.
The cop followed them as they drove away, and stayed
with them at every turn. Finally they went home and hung
out quietly until the cop car drove off. By the time they got
to the park, Gerry was huddled up shivering by the trunk of
a Norway maple, afraid to walk home dressed like a thief, his
adrenalin-induced arrhythmia failing to keep him warm.
He was half-asleep when he heard the minivan. He
jumped up, ran to it, and pounded on the back as they passed.
"Gerry?" Zoëy whispered when they stopped. They
opened the rear sliding door and he climbed in. "Did you get
any animals?"
Gerry burst out laughing. He couldn't help it. He was
soaked and covered in mud and blood and hadn't come within
a hundred metres of a live animal except the dogs on Tower
Road howling at picture windows.
He looked at Zoëy's serious face, concerned though he
couldn't tell if it was for him or the animals. He tried to mirror
her stoicism on his own face. He'd been afraid since finding
the door locked in the lab basement that the futility of this effort would not only erase her respect for him, but his for her.
He needn't have worried. This approach was all wrong, trying to attack systematic cruelty with a hammer and chisel and
balaclava and minivan. But her intentions were pure. Operation Niblet had failed but she would change the world and he
would be right there with her.
"The door was locked," he said. "Couldn't get in at all."
Before she could answer he leaned forward and kissed her.
When she kissed back, as if trying to douse a flame with her
spit, his heart slowed for the first time since climbing into the
lab's basement.

In the weeks following the failure of Operation Niblet,
Terry, Sue, and Zoëy tried to convince him to have another go

at the lab, and that their inside person could take care of that unexpected locked door, and that usually security was nowhere near the lab between 3:00 and 4:00 and it must have been a busy night on campus or something.

He didn't regret his actions. They gave him the courage or the rush he needed to kiss Zoëy. But busting animals loose from the joint wasn't his style. He was more a thinker, and an artist. The failed caper and subsequent fumbling through Zoëy's loose clothing to her skin inspired several new paintings, all pounded into canvas while Zoëy slept after their intense fucking, during which their hands groped at every curve and seam in an attempt to become one multi-orgasmic body. Gerry couldn't sleep afterward; he was jolted awake by the intensity of her legs wrapped around him and he shook as he painted with the urgency of night, the need to finish before dawn.

The paintings weren't obvious interpretations of animal rights or love or the clear association between the two in Gerry's mind. They were pictures of dew on spider webs and piglets running through dandelions, waves exploding on rocks, and other snippets of glory etched in his memory by orgasm. Such pictures had no more hope of changing the world than smoking a joint and shooting the shit on the porch, he realized, but they came more naturally to him. And he feared going to jail, alone, having to find another new identity in order to fit in with another new group. He'd rather stay here with Zoëy.

The paintings were his only answer to Zoëy's escalating demands for radical action of some sort. He'd nod and kiss her and go down on her until she forgot about non-human animals and he'd paint the rest of the night.

The more they fucked the more radicalized she became – the more obsessed with proving to him that a revolution could work – and the more she ranted on revolution the more obsessed he became with fucking her. She gave him books about the world's great revolutions and he bought her a copy of the *Kama Sutra*. When she asked him to consider what would be lost if they did nothing, he took it as a threat to stop fucking him.

"All right," he told her, "tell me about your revolution then." He hoped she had something better than a bigger and crazier version of Niblet. As she spooned him, he felt safe and protected – as he'd once felt with his high school buddies – and he knew that happiness is something so elusive a man will do anything to keep it once he's found it. He laughed aloud. A bigger and crazier version of Operation Niblet was exactly what he was going to get.

DELIA AND PHIL

Delia's older than Phil, less stable but more fun. Phil, though not completely satisfied, knows it's True Love because he enjoys spending money on Delia that he doesn't really have. Delia accepts his gifts without a thought. She loves pinching Phil's ass in public, chasing behind him with two fingers firmly holding denim and a chunk of his glutinous flesh, the two laughing hysterically all the way to the station.

On the bus they argue about what to do next. Delia wants them go see her mother. Phil hates Delia's mother and prefers to go to the movies alone while Delia's at her mother's.

Phil's hatred of Delia's mother stems from class-warfare propaganda spewed by his father, a bitter seed planted in Phil when he was a fetus. Phil's father was a union man, and the only things he hated more than people richer than himself were people more powerful than himself. For Phil, Delia's mother falls into both these categories. The influence Phil's father's class-based politics has had on Phil's life is amazing when you consider that Phil's dad left him and his mother when Phil was only seven years old. Before the boy had ever spoken a word.

From Phil's father's perspective, the only thing he could have spawned more embarrassing than Phil would have been a rich baby. Sure, there was honour in raising a retard, but honour was a whole lot of work, and Phil's father worked hard enough already. It was better to leave the nurturing of a Down's kid to a woman, who is designed for such things.

Phil's father sent a cheque every other month in the mail, with no return address on the envelope. When the cheques arrived, Phil's mother would buy him some sweets at the store, and she'd always say, "It's a present from Daddy." Phil idolized his absent father.

But as much as he loved his candy and his father, they were mere heartburn compared to the all-consuming fire of adoration Phil had for his mother in the early years. Phil's mother went to work when her husband left, replacing him at the factory on the coveted eight-hour day shift. Phil's father's boss, whom Phil's father had hated for his power, took pity on the single mom of a Down's kid, even though he knew the company would have to pay for daycare, an extra-expensive "special" one at that.

Every morning when his mother dropped him off at the special daycare for special kids, Phil cried. The staff members there were not special, but specialized, and they slowly and arduously taught Phil to speak clearly, and even read a bit.

Phil's mom was home by five each evening with Phil in tow. It was Phil's favourite hour. After a hard day of enunciation practice, his slowly erased energy magically reappeared in the form of his mother beaming open-armed at the door. He'd tear away from whatever picture book he was reading and run straight into her embrace. It was the most focused and direct his teachers ever saw him.

The next four hours of the day were filled with uninterrupted games. "I Spy" on the way home, "Tag" on the way inside the house, a tickle-off in the hallway, food fights while she made dinner and again while they ate. And then off he went to his own marvellous games: building Lego cities, making superheroes out of teddy bears, racing cars around the apartment. And when things got dull, erecting fortresses of cushions, impenetrable by any soldier, be he a toy or an invisible construction of the mind.

Every night before she started crying, Phil's mom put an

exhausted but happy little boy to bed. It was like that until puberty, when Phil became another surly and distant teenaged boy, avalanching his mother with strong words whenever she got too close or made too much noise.

The problem with Phil's mother was that she thought just because he had Down's, that made him a baby forever. Little did Phil realize that this baby treatment was common to mothers whether their babies were autistic, athletic, brilliant, or broken. Four or forty-four. Phil had been her sunlight in a world of indoor punch cards; she missed the little boy who ran full-tilt toward her at five each evening and jarred her with the thrust of his entire little body. Reminding her the world was still alive and so was she.

What Phil did realize was that his mother did not believe he would ever be self-sufficient, with a grade six reading level, and it angered him so much that he quit high school, where he was in the special class once again. He got himself a job at SD Inc., sorting mail by department and delivering it to the appropriate offices.

Phil found the job a lot like school. He had to force himself to concentrate and sometimes he didn't see the point of it, but when he did it well he felt pretty good about himself. He wondered what his officemates thought of him. He sensed that some of them really liked having him around, and others acted like they did, but they didn't. A few were outright hostile. Phil preferred the people who were hostile to those who pretended to like him.

The mail was late the day Phil met Delia. Phil was mad and shouted to no one in particular that the goddamn mail carrier should be fired. Most of his co-workers in the mailroom and surrounding offices politely ignored him, with two notable exceptions.

The first exception was Phil's boss, who scolded him: "Phil, you can't yell like that in here."

"Leave me the *hell* alone!" Phil said.

The other notable response to Phil's outrage came from Delia. Running in with the mail, she heard Phil cursing the mail carrier. It was her first day on a new route and she'd gotten lost. It usually took her a while to get used to a new route. She ran to Phil and handed him the day's mail. "I'm sorry I'm late, sir," she said sweetly. "I got lost."

Phil took the bag from her hands as if it contained hydrogen, flint, and lighter fluid. He stared at her the whole time, taking in her broad nose, thin lips, wispy hair, far-apart eyes. She wasn't pretty like his mom, but she had a kind face. And no one had ever called him "sir" before. Phil turned slowly and wordlessly from her, dumped the mail into a bin, and began sorting. Delia rushed out and hurried to her next delivery. Both began counting the hours to their next meeting.

Delia was planning so carefully for when she saw Phil again that she got lost three more times that day, and only just made her final delivery, at 4:30, when the office buildings were closing. Then it was home, to try in vain to keep her mother sober.

She was already drunk when Delia got there, as was often the case. It was the case during Delia's birth and the two-year period leading up to it. It used to be the case for Delia's father until he moved next door. According to Delia's mother, it was her husband who drove her to drink. According to Delia's father, it was her mother's drinking that drove him to leave. Delia believed both of them.

Delia spent a few hours that night listening to her mother say terrible things about her father, nodding sympathetically all the while. Even in a drunken stupor, Delia's mother was a servant the likes of which would make Jesus jealous, offering milk, cake, pie with cream, tea, and hot chocolate, none of which Delia wanted.

"Sit still, Mother," Delia urged in her patient drawl, sounding halfway drunk herself. "Why don't we just sit and talk?"

"Talk about what?"

"Well, Mother, I met a boy – a man – today."

Mother looked at her blankly.

Delia gazed back the same way.

"And?"

Delia didn't know what to say. She thought the point had been made. "Isn't that enough for you?" she blurted, just as Mother was losing her patience. The words had inertia in their favour, being on their way out anyway, so she just set them free.

"No, it's not enough! It's barely a sentence. You met a man? That's it? I met several men today, Dee, women too. It's what I do." Delia's mother was a top sales rep with a major music distributor. "Kiddo, you wonder why I want to help you when you're so helpless! You come home two hours late and all you can say is you met a man. You can't even communicate!"

Unlike Phil and his mom, Delia and her mother had never had a good relationship. There was, however, a time when their fights were more engaging: more involved and more detailed. Things used to progress slowly, starting with Delia politely accepting her mother's pies and cakes, until she looked down to see crumbs on her fat blouse and became filled with self-loathing. Then she'd politely refuse a third helping, at which point her mother would check her forehead for fever and, finding a normal temperature, refill her daughter's plate. "I'm full, Mother," Delia would groan softly.

"Oh, sweetie," her mother would answer. "Why deny yourself the only sensual pleasure you have in life? Don't worry about the outside. You're beautiful inside, that's what counts."

Once Delia learned the meaning of the word "sensual" her mother was in big trouble, but even that developed slowly. "I have sensual pleasure," she said proudly one evening.

"Oh, really?" Her mother's eyebrow rose and her chin tilted downwards.

"Yep."

"From whom?"

"Huh?"

"Who gives you this sensual pleasure?"

"You do, Mother."

"Don't be saucy!"

"It's true! Your voice is music to my ears."

"Eat your cake, dearie."

"I'm watching my figure," said Delia, in the style of a '50s television housewife, openly and proudly, yet with a submissive undertone.

"What figure, honey? You're not like other girls."

"I'm a woman, Mother."

"What kind of woman are you, Delia? What kind of woman eats her mother's cake all day, never cleans, has no husband or lover, no job? What kind of woman has to be reminded to wipe after she pees?"

"I do not!"

Delia's mother started listing her daughter's limitations until Delia backed down and offered her a drink. This was the routine for several years, until one day her mother decided to break through the pattern's pretty ceiling. As she accepted her drink, she said, "You know, honey, the way you stress me out and then calm me with martinis, well, it'll be your fault if my liver falls on the floor one day."

"Well, it's your fault I'm like this!" was the reply, and it became Delia's mantra. Like *this* like this like *this* – oh God, like this like this. "This" being small-eyed and cleft-lipped, simple, slow, fat, and unappealing.

On the west side of Delia's room was a wide window; outside, five feet away, there was a large east-facing window. Connecting them was the door from an old shed, lying flat between the two window sills. The shed had long since died of loneliness, collapsing from neglect in the shared backyard. After an argument with her mother, Delia would crawl across the old door and into the window of her father's bedroom, which he never inhabited.

Invariably she'd find him downstairs, in the living room, embedded in his old grey couch, either napping or watching the television news. She'd plop herself down on the floor in front of his head with a loud sigh, either waking him or blocking his view.

Despite his knowledge of the source of her sigh, he always asked, "What's wrong, Radish?" Plenty of fathers called their daughters cutesy food names like Pumpkin or Cupcake, but only her old man could make Radish sound sweet. It was his favourite vegetable.

"Mother and I had a fight."

"She call you fat?"

"Yeah."

"Bitch."

"Daaa-deeeee."

"Why don't you move in here with me, Radish? I promise I'll never call you fat."

This conversation with her father was not so much its own routine as an extension of the routine fight with her mother. Routine was Delia's foundation. She managed by breaking life into small pieces, and practising each bit until it was easy. She repeated them until some external force made her do otherwise, like this new route. Despite the illusion of autonomy, each thing she did was an identically shaped piece of a linear puzzle, unique only in the amount of time it took her to carry it out.

"You know I can't."

Like her arguments with Mother, the conversations with Daddy had been refined and streamlined over time, with practice. Where once he would probe and inquire as to the nature of his wife's insults and his daughter's retorts, now he started with the question of fat, made his offer, and accepted her rejection. Then he made another offer, the comfort of having her hair played with as they watched a movie, before she returned to her mother's house and found her room for the evening.

On the day of Delia and Phil's second meeting, she didn't get lost once on her way to SD Inc. She took the mail directly to Phil, who was relieved it was on time and intrigued by Delia's reappearance.

"What happened to Sam?" he asked. Sam was her predecessor, a crotchety old bastard who was egalitarian in his distaste for all living things. The only things he hated slightly more than everything else were dogs, viruses, and Phil.

"He retired," she informed him.

"Good," Phil said. He had been hoping Sam died.

"Yes, he's a nice man."

"No, he's not," Phil said. "You're nicer."

Delia blushed at the unexpected compliment. Phil went to his sorting, leaving her standing there without a word in her mouth.

Again the two played heavily on each other's thoughts for the rest of the day, though neither would have guessed the interest was mutual. Delia got lost three more times on the last part of her route.

Between the two of them, Phil was the more predictable. Ever since his father left his mother, the Special Kid Specialists had cultivated for Phil a one-temperature climate in a four-season environment. Phil's mother tried to keep it one hundred percent sweet by sheltering him from cold, hunger, poverty, freak storms, temper tantrums, delays, and death – sheltering him, in effect, from life. In a word, he was spoiled. He was chauffeured everywhere and kept indoors; his life with his mom was a series of games and good food and short trips. With organizational skills that would make most corporate secretaries envious, she calendared Phil's life into identical blocks that repeated themselves over and over for eighteen years, by which time Phil expected things to happen in the same manner perpetually. If his mom could do it, why couldn't the Canadian postal system? Why couldn't SD Inc.?

To Phil, Delia was a wild woman. As crotchety as Sam had been, Phil appreciated and counted on the man's to-the-minute regularity, his neatly pressed uniform, his combed moustache and hair. Delia's hair looked like it was trying to fly away, or as if some other flying thing had collected it into a loosely made nest. And once she got used to the new route, her deliveries arrived with temporal variances of up to thirty minutes. She broadened Phil's horizon to the point where he could repress his rage at the shift in routine, but only because he was fascinated by her beauty, which was increasing for him daily.

Delia was captivated enough to break one of her routines too, one week after their first encounter. On that night when her father asked her "What's wrong, Radish?" she answered, "I'm in love, Daddy."

So habitual was their routine that he answered, "She call you fat?"

Delia turned and stared into his face. Her bewilderment confused him, and he repeated the question.

"I said I'm in love, Daddy."

He blinked twice. "With what?"

"A man."

"What kind of man?"

"A mail-sorting man."

"At work?"

"SD Inc."

Delia's father blinked three more times and said, "What's his name?"

"I don't know."

It dawned on him that his thirty-one-year-old daughter had just developed her first crush – that he knew of anyway. "How old is he?" He bided his time, unsure of the situation and his place within it. He hadn't felt that way about his relationship with Delia since he'd bought and moved into the house next door fifteen years earlier.

"I don't know, Daddy. I don't know anything about him. Except he's cute, and he has a nice bum." She giggled. Her father heaved a relieved sigh. It was less complicated than he'd feared.

"Cute with nice bum isn't love, Radish. That's the same mistake I made with your mother."

"Daddy – gross!"

"*Excuse* me, Radish. God forbid *I* have a sex drive, at my age." The sentence came out easily, naturally, like it would for many fathers talking to their grown daughters, but once the words were in the air, destined for her ears, they served as an awkward reminder of how unlike other father-daughter relationships theirs was, and he felt perverted. The word *sex* had never been uttered by either of them, not when they were together, anyway. "Sorry," he muttered.

"That's okay, Daddy." She took a breath. "Mommy called me fat."

"Bitch."

She smiled, comforted.

"So are you going to ask this boy on a date?"

"Oh, I couldn't. He wouldn't like me."

"Why the hell not? What kind of lowly son of a bitch wouldn't like my lovely Delia?"

"I'm fat. And slow."

"You're beautiful. And a carrier of Canadian mail. You never miss a day of work, never mind a delivery." A lie, but a nice compliment, so she didn't debate the point. "That's good, noble work. Any man worth his salt would be honoured by the attentions of a woman like you."

Though her father had been reaching high for compliments, because he loved her and believed her to be wonderful if unaccomplished, his words played in her mind like battle trumpets as she approached Phil. *You are a carrier of the*

Canadian mail. You are beautiful. If she could show up on time every day, and deliver every coupon, invoice, and pink slip to every stop on time (almost), surely she could ask this boy out.

"Sir," she said, handing him his mail, "I have something to ask you. You see, well, I've noticed that, well, to be honest ... anyway ... you see. You see?"

Not only did he not see, Phil was getting agitated. He'd been holding SD Inc. mail for almost two minutes and not sorted a single piece, yet he couldn't turn away from this blathering bird-nest-headed beauty. He shook his head to indicate his confusion.

"Well, I really like delivering mail to you. I like seeing you, I mean. I was wondering if you'd like to come to a puppet show with me. This weekend."

"A puppet show?"

"Yeah! There's one every Saturday afternoon at the library, just down the road from here."

"My mom used to take me when I was a kid. But now I'm grown up."

"Oh, you're never too old for puppets. Some of the people that go are as old as my parents."

"Yeah, the grandparents of the kids maybe."

"Well, yeah, but they like the puppets just as much as the kids do."

Phil was averse to games and toys. He liked to work hard, go home to his bachelor apartment, and watch the news and sports. Sometimes he would surf the Internet on the computer he'd bought with his own money. His independent living counsellor had helped him get connected. On weekends Phil drank coffee, read the paper, and followed a set regimen of educational television programming. He liked his routine. It was as set and scheduled as his childhood, but without the childish things. Now here was this talking bird's nest trying to break his routine and expose him to toys, children's entertainment.

"Okay, I'll go," he said.

"Great!" She was breathless, spit the confirmation out before he could come to his senses and take it back. In moments he was receiving a pamphlet with the time and location and her number scrawled on it just in case, which she was cramming into his pants pocket. He mumbled about looking forward to seeing her at the library. As he turned, he felt her hand squeeze his ass. He froze.

Delia let go. What did I just do? she asked herself, knowing the answer, knowing she'd blown it. As she mentally prepared her Official Statement of Apology, he turned back to her and she saw, lo and behold, a smile on his face – a big toothy grin. She chuckled.

Phil's mother used to do that, until he'd made her stop a few months before he moved out. She did it in that same flirtatious, playful, spontaneous, asexual way that had never failed to elicit a bucktoothed grin from him until he was seventeen years old and as crotchety as an old man waiting to retire or die.

Delia gave Phil a goodbye smile and a wink and sauntered away, amazed at her flirtatiousness, wondering where her boldness had come from.

When she told her father these things, he replied, with some astonishment, that her mother had done something very similar when she'd first asked him out. Now he was concerned. What if, after all these years of nice quiet evenings together conspiring against his wife, Delia suddenly grew up? What if she ran off and married this man?

His fears were based on his idea of Phil, which he soon learned was nothing like the reality. The Phil he imagined was much like Phil's idea of Phil: mature, manly, downright professional. The real Phil *loved* the puppet show. The real Phil fell hard for Delia and the fun she provided, but he was too fearful of reverting to a state of complete dependence on a woman to show it. Phil, like most men, was still a boy despite the image he believed in and tried to project.

His first meeting with Delia's mother was a disaster, falling miles short of Delia's mental image of Phil slam-dunking a basketball over her helpless mother's head. Delia's mother simply couldn't fathom her daughter's decision to waste her first romance on someone even more *lagging* than she was. Phil took her condescending tone as a symptom of snobbery, and he told Delia so.

Delia cried, although she couldn't care less about class. She was sad because her mother had not eaten her words about her daughter's being unlovable. Now here was Phil being defensive, and making her feel as unlovable as the woman who had borne and raised her always maintained she was. When Delia cried, she reminded Phil even more of his poor mother, and his guilt at leaving her, and never calling.

Despite Delia's mother, and the spectre of his, Phil can often be seen running with a big toothy grin on his face, Delia's fingers firmly planted on the right cheek of his ass, laughing, giving chase. Sometimes it's near the bus stop after a brief argument about visiting Delia's mother. After they decide to go to the movies instead, Delia tells him she's picking up the tab.

INEVITABLE

Wanda thought of death under the Superstore's white lights. They brought to mind a corpse. She hurried out of the all-naturals aisle and rear-ended a man's cart with hers. He was standing to the side looking at flower arrangements at the end of a very long lineup for the cashier. Wanda ground her teeth as the carts collided. "Shit. Sorry. Wow, what a line."

"No problem," he said. He smiled. The incandescence of the neon light sparkled off his blue eyes.

She smiled back. "What a line. Looks like I'll miss *Jeopardy*."

"Chance encounters for a thousand, Alex."

She gave a split-second gasp, which encouraged him. He mistook it for a laugh.

"Belly laughs for two thousand."

"Big charmers for three thousand." Why was she was playing along?

"I don't think they go up to three thousand on that show."

"True."

"Maybe we should get together and watch." He smiled and smoothed down his moustache with two fingers.

The moustache was, weirdly, reminiscent of Alex Trebek's, before he shaved it. He was decent looking. Wanda figured him for a fuck-up. She was not an appealing person.

"Or we could have dinner. Like at a restaurant," he said.

Like at a restaurant? "Um." Wanda spun and strode back down the aisle.

He shouted something after her, brief and trite, then thought to introduce himself. "I'm Al! By the way. I didn't catch your name."

"Wanda!" She didn't look back. She did a 180 at the end of the aisle and sprinted through the produce section toward the exit.

"You forgot your groceries, Wanda."

She'd have to go back later, which would throw off her routine and mess up her sleep. She'd be a hundred percent ruined in the morning.

Wanda was submersed naked in the South China Sea, eyes open and headed toward bioluminescence. The deeps pushed the weight of an elephant on each of her too-many square millimetres, but the pressure provided cocoon-like comfort. She was warm and cozy exploring what few have seen. There was one nagging cold spot, her nose. It felt singularly wet, though her body was underwater. There was a high yowl over the deep sea's furnace-like white noise. There was a weight on her chest, that wetness of nose, and fur in her eyes.

"Wichita?"

The cat confirmed with another yowl.

"What time is it?"

Wanda pushed Wichita to the floor, rolled onto her side, and checked the clock. 6:30. She closed her eyes and tried to remember bioluminescence, imagining a six-foot eel – columns of razor teeth – as the source of light. She pulled the blanket over her head to seal out the cold. Wichita's claws sank through the blanket to her skin. Wanda wondered if life might be easier if her cat starved to death. She reached for the softwood floor to knock on it, protecting herself, and Wichita, from the horrible thought. Long before her mother died, death – the fear of it – had stalked her. But since that loss she could feel death's presence, hear its creaky longings. It wanted her. It wanted everyone. Decay and breakdown are inevitable.

Everybody thinks of death. Wanda saw it everywhere, going after people's skulls, their blood bubbling through their skin as if through a waffle grid. Her response was to scratch behind her right ear. Sometimes her mind's eye would wander back there and see her scratching and flaking off layer after layer of skin until, again, a bloody grid appeared. Then she pulled at her long hair until a few came out – real hairs, not mind's-eye hairs – and she'd go back to scratching, this time at her arms, leaving real red blotches that occasionally got bloody. Or she'd knock on her head like it was wood, keeping bad thoughts at bay. She knocked harder and harder until she was punching herself, trying to knock these torturing images out of there.

She could see and feel and do these things with her eyes closed, no visual stimulation needed. She'd see her scalp and be powerless to stop herself from feeling the line where hair meets skin. She'd see the skin peel back, revealing brain matter; she'd see microscopic views of flakes of skin inhabiting her hair. When she had a sore joint she could feel the place where bone meets bone, the thinner fragments connecting, the air popping when she cracked her knuckles, the muscle stretching and blood pulsing when she moved. She was deteriorating slowly toward death. These things disgusted and scared her – how easily things could be broken or knocked out of place, letting other things fall out or be infected.

Once she got started down this thought path, little could stop her. Sleep would keep her from abusing herself but it brought bad dreams. Work helped but was its own form of torture. Her job as an acupuncturist's bookkeeper let her avoid all but the most cursory of interactions with people but it was tedious and she longed for the skill to engage in a normal conversation with someone besides Dr. Colbourne, who didn't have much to say to her beyond the numbers.

Wanda found her way to the kitchen and pulled Wichita's vet-prescribed diet food from the cupboard. As she lowered a scoopful to his dish, Wichita whacked her hand with claws extended. She dropped the food and scoop. He attacked the food open-mouthed as if she might steal it back, his fierce belly swinging.

"You're more likely to die of a heart attack than starvation." She knocked on her head three times and put rubbing alcohol on her wounds. God knew what kind of bacteria Wichita carried. At least he was an indoor cat.

Though she got up early, Wanda was late for work. There'd been a new issue of *S&M E-monthly* in her inbox. She'd become engrossed in a story of a sadist Irish Traveller in a dungeon-mistress competition. The e-mag left her no time for breakfast, which would lead to overeating at lunch. She was grateful that the bus stopped a hundred metres from her house. The last thing she needed was some Monday morning still-drunk driver to veer his hatchback into her. She knocked on her head at the thought, but couldn't shake it and kept pounding, re-bruising her knuckles. Idiot drivers were why she kept Wichita indoors.

On the bus someone called her name. A vaguely familiar male voice. She looked up to see him wave from the back. The guy from the grocery store. Joel? She held up her hand and let it go limp at the wrist. This guy, aggressively nice. Clearly wanted sex. Sex with another person, in real life, was a thought rotted with potential disease. She didn't need this. If she hadn't messed around all morning she'd be at work instead of stuck on the commuter line with this guy. Alan? He beckoned her with an uppercut wave and pointed at the vacant seat next to him.

"Al," he said, extending his hand. "Remember?"

"Yes. Young Street Superstore."

She shook his hand and resisted the urge to pull a wet-nap

from her purse. Al and Wanda together again, under another set of neon white lights.

"You were sure in a hurry. At the store."

"The Young Street Superstore. I was. Sorry. Thought I'd left a burner on. But ..."

"False alarm?"

She nodded until she noticed him nodding too. He looked ridiculous so she stopped.

"So, you never answered my question. About dinner?"

"Oh." She nodded again and forced herself to stop. "Look ..."

"Oh. That's okay."

"Sorry. It's not you it's ... my viruses."

Al tilted his head sideways to an unnatural angle and kind of smirked and squinted simultaneously. "Viruses?"

She couldn't go through with the lie. It felt bigger than she'd expected. "Well. Computer viruses."

"Oh. I can fix your virus problem. I'm in IT."

Wanda nodded.

She really did have a computer-virus problem. She'd lost two computers to them. Probably because of the porn sites. She used to watch a lot. It made her ... not happy, but thinking about sex – consuming it, staring at it – induced a state of mindless Zen. It was all consuming. She didn't worry until afterward, when she got viruses. So, a few months after buying a new computer, she subscribed to S&M E-monthly. Still, the new computer got slower, crashed more. She didn't know anybody in IT. Until Al. She gave him her number. When he called, she skipped the small talk and invited him over. He arrived wearing the cutest, cleanest denim overalls and a short-sleeved, collared white dress shirt, also spotless.

She led him through the kitchen and up a spiral staircase. Wichita followed at her heels and made several clumsy attempts to rub her moving feet, forcing her into a side-to-side jig that made Al chuckle. She pointed at her desktop. "There he is: Hal. The demon computer from hell." She pursed her lips, unsure what else to say. "It feels like it's against me. The pop-ups. Ugh." She shrugged. "I'll leave you to it." She scooped up Wichita on her way out.

Al came downstairs more than an hour later. "So, you like it rough?"

Her eyes darted upward, off Jason Priestley's teenaged television antics and onto this rude interruption. "Excuse me?"

"Um, porn. Free music too. You have a lot of downloads. That's where the viruses and the pop-ups are coming from."

Her face caught fire.

"Didn't mean to embarrass you. It's a common source of viruses. There are safer sites you can go to."

"Sure. I have one. I don't use free ones anymore."

"But you used to. It's probably been sick a while." Al stopped talking and lurched at her, lips puckered like Tweety Bird's beak.

Wanda dodged him and jumped up from her La-Z-Boy.

He fell into it face first and pushed himself back up. "Rough is okay with me. You can hit me. If you want to."

She nodded toward the door. "Get out. Thanks for the computer help, but please get the fuck out."

He dusted himself off like a cowboy in a western, tipped his imaginary hat, and stomped out the door.

Al had installed a different anti-virus program, something she'd never heard of, a spyware detector and a new firewall. He'd done something else too. She didn't know what but Hal was much quicker.

Wanda went straight for *S&M E-monthly*, but she'd already read the latest issue. She usually logged on as a distraction and worked her way to horny. But damn Al – that weirdo, that probable sociopath, likely crawling with germs – his offensive behaviour had turned her on. No one had ever come on to her like that before. Asshole.

Wanda tried rereading a story about an office boy being sexually harassed by the human resources team (and loving it). It wasn't doing it for her. She took her clothes off and turned the fan on. Maybe the breeze would stimulate her. She stood in front of the mirror thinking of Al. She wondered again what he might see in her. She was pretty enough. She'd always imagined that if she had a best friend, that person would describe her as "pleasantly plump" or some other banal backhanded-at-best compliment, only they would say it with genuine love. This best friend would tell her that she could be really attractive if she looked people in the eye and didn't walk around punching herself in the head.

She imagined Al as the office boy in the *S&M E-monthly* story and spoke aloud to him. "Al, my computer is frozen again; *come* fix it. Pronto, Al. I have a meeting in five minutes and I need to print off a report. If you'd fixed it right last time, Al, I wouldn't be so screwed. You want me to be screwed, Al?"

She imagined Al rushing to fix the problem, bending over the keyboard, and pounding on it with his fingers like a digital Liberace. She'd call him incompetent, insult his overalls and dress shirt. He'd be chipper as she slapped his butt and accused *him* of harassment. He'd put his hands in his pockets to hide his erection as he returned to his cubicle.

Al left several apology messages. "Sorry I came on so strong. Sorry I'm so clumsy. I like you. I thought you'd like it. I'm an ass. I've never had a charming sort of, like, way with women."

S&M E-monthly started to seem like a waste of money. She had to reimagine every story with Al as the star. Finally she answered one of his calls. She wasn't in a forgiving mood yet. She pressed talk and before he could say anything she shouted at him. "Not only did you find all the old sites I thought I deleted. You also watched it!"

"Only a little. There was a lot of it. It was a lot of work getting rid of it all without deleting any of your personal photos and stuff."

"You're proud of it."

He didn't answer. It was the first moment of silence they'd shared. He seemed the type to not allow pauses in conversation, cutting other people off if necessary to avoid the risk of quiet.

"I assume your computer is working better now."

She hated him for infecting her with an incurable image of his butt on her La-Z-Boy after he'd tried pitifully to kiss her.

"I could strangle you, Al."

"Tell me about it, Wanda."

"I could wrap both hands around your scrawny neck and squeeze."

"Go on."

She wanted to punch him.

"Go ahead, tell me."

She invited him over. When he arrived, he was awkward but less pushy after a couple glasses of wine. Still nice. He helped wash the dishes and snuggled with Wichita as Wanda told him about her mother's unexpected death. Wanda had Vivaldi playing because it soothed her nerves. In another moment of silence, Al stood and swayed and spun with his arms out, like a drunken scarecrow with innate rhythm. She hadn't known it was possible to dance like that to Vivaldi. He invited her to join him. Such passion delighted and scared her. It was the same feeling she got when the kids on her street pelted one another with snowballs.

She was amazed when he kissed her goodnight. The kiss was delicious and somewhat repulsive, but she was fine after a good brush and gargle. Weeks of fantasy proved far from reality. She spent much of the night wanting to ask him what he saw in her but she never worked up the courage. He visited her frequently for two months before they had sex. When it was over he looked at the ceiling with a stupid frown on his face.

She apologized. "I shouldn't have made you take a shower first." She made herself spoon him. His chest rose and fell and she imagined clothespins attached to his small dark nipples.

He took a deep breath and held it for what seemed an impossible length of time. She poked his belly and he spit the air out.

"It wasn't at all like what I saw on your computer."

She rolled away, thinking of showering again. "You shouldn't have looked at that."

"Those women seemed so excited."

"If I did the stuff in those videos to you? It could kill you."

"Now you're worried about *my* death?"

It was good to have a friend, but the arguments were hard work. They centred on sex and death. She wouldn't go across town to his place. The more time you spend in traffic the more likely you are to be in an accident. Even on a bus. Al came over and they watched TV, petted the cat. She wanted him, badly, but not the way she had once fantasized. He wanted her, badly, exactly as she had once fantasized. She didn't want to hurt him. He was delicate, vulnerable, and needy – like Wichita. It had all been sugar and sunshine until they screwed. They compromised, after *Jeopardy*, with a mechanical fuck and another conversation about death.

"I know how you're going to die anyway," he said. "You're going to be so distracted imagining your own death you're going to walk in front of a moving bus."

She punched his chest and he whimpered. He promised her he could handle anything she might do to him. "You could put both your thumbs on my Adam's apple and push. You could pop it. I wouldn't complain."

She winced. Was that his idea of a turn-on? But she snuggled closer to him, determined to resolve things.

She rubbed his nipples and bit his shoulder, first a nibble, then she put her jaw into it, heard him inhale sharply, watched him writhe. What if she did what she really wanted? If she slapped him around. Pulled back her fist and punched his mouth. So hard his head snapped back. So hard he bled. Lost a tooth. What if she really, really hurt him, sped up the inevitability of his death? What if she were merely cruel? Would he cry if she called him a little shit? If she threatened him? She rolled over on top of him. Put her hands on his throat and squeezed. Gently. His eyes bulged. She saw fear and eased her grip so he could breathe, a little.

"It's okay," he grunted.

She let go. "Here." She turned her back to him, leaned forward, and spread her legs over his face. As she lowered herself onto his mouth she saw Wichita watching them from the floor. She pushed herself hard over Al's mouth and nose, pinned his head and shoulders to the mattress with her thighs and knees, until he gasped into her. Her body shook as a white neon light exploded behind her eyes and she thought of nothing.

HOME

He strides across the hippie diner toward her, hand extended, mispronouncing her name slightly. He pronounces it "Buyer Ma."

"Are you Dan?"

"I figured it was you, going by the name."

She smiles. She is practically Canadian now.

"Ready to see the place?"

"Yes, sir."

"Out back." Dan walks down the aisle. He steps on a dropped soother as he passes a young mother breastfeeding her infant. He doesn't break stride, doesn't seem to notice the pacifier under his sneaker.

Bayarmaa follows Dan through a grey metallic side door and up a flight of wooden stairs with jagged lettering all over it – some of it carved and some inked. She recognizes a variation on the famous Robert Frost line about the road less travelled, in black spray paint, next to a blood-red swastika.

They come to a hallway with three doors. Dan sticks the key in the middle door and opens it. There is a small room, or a large closet, with a desk and a single futon on the floor, off-white with yellower stains. It has a large vertical window with no curtain or blinds. She looks out the window.

"It's a great view," Dan says.

It isn't bad. She can see the bridge but not the water under it. And it's quiet, sturdy enough to keep out the noises from the street and restaurant. "Where's the bathroom? And kitchen? And laundry?"

"Basement. All in the basement."

She follows him back down the stairs, this time noticing how steep they are, how loose the thin wooden railing is. Outside there is a concrete set of steps going down to a door, which Dan opens. "This is Del's apartment. He's a cool dude – a drummer. He's really made it his own."

Bayarmaa's eyes are slow to adjust to the darkness. "Can you turn a light on?"

Dan laughs. "I did. Del likes it dark though."

A lamp covered by a black shade is lit in the middle of the apartment. The objects in the apartment are divided in groups according to what room you'd expect to find them in – an open toilet and bathtub in one area, a stove, beer fridge, and sink full of dishes in another area, futon, coffee table, and lamp in the middle, with drum pieces lying around. But there are no walls separating these things. Bayarmaa wonders how she is supposed to use the bathroom when Del is home. Is he supposed to leave his apartment every time she has to relieve herself?

"Well," Dan says, "it ain't much but what can you expect for the price?"

She expects more. Like a washer and dryer, notably absent.

"Laundromat's three blocks north."

Once she's on the street again she sees things she should have noticed on the way in, obvious things like the couple sitting on the sidewalk next to a shopping cart full of bulging garbage bags, the two of them yelling slurred words back and forth. And the men in front of the shelter smoking something foul.

She walks away from the harbour, back up toward the Common, where her second cousins live. She had hoped to never see them again. She doesn't like the way they stay up late drinking vodka on the couch, which is where she sleeps when she can. Bayarmaa has to stay there another night.

She spends three more nights on her cousins' couch before she finds an apartment she can barely afford. It's nothing special and it is stressful paying more that she budgeted, but it has what she needs and at least she doesn't have to walk through anyone else's space to go pee. She imagines standing in the cold, pounding on Del the drummer's door with a full bladder.

The mold at the new place is disconcerting and it's cold living in the basement. The woman who owns the house, an artist with several cats and a bewildered fish, is kind and lets her use the washer and dryer.

Across the road is a compound of apartment buildings. They remind her of her old Soviet building, back when she worked for the Bank of Mongolia in Ulaanbaatar. Much bigger city than Halifax. And colder. Her building was a monolithic grate of vertical concrete, punctured by pockets of glass, built over permafrost. An imperialist postcard. From her window she could see the suburbs, which were comprised nearly entirely of sprawling little white yurts. The sight of them took her back to her early childhood, following Mother around to help milk the livestock and leading little sisters about gathering dried dung for fuel. When she left, her parents made it clear she was not to come home without a driver, a personal assistant, and the cash to pay back the loans they'd taken for her schooling.

One thing she likes about the new place is watching the liveliness of the compound across the street, which has a large rectangular common area in the middle where children run around throwing snowballs at each other, wrestling or kicking a half-inflated soccer ball across the ice. Sometimes some of the parents join in the games. The families are mostly Black. It's nice to see people watching each other's kids. That happened sometimes when she was a child, but only rarely, when the adults weren't busy herding or milking or butchering the animals.

Mongolian government men promised her the world

through education and now here she is. She did well in junior management at the Bank of Mongolia, researching and monitoring policies to maintain a stable currency, but everyone told her if she wanted to make any real money she had to be in North America. The currency she worked to stabilize wasn't worth much in the wider world. She has to start over here, work her way back up to the middle. She submitted hundreds of résumés as soon as she arrived and was granted not a single interview, not even for the jobs for which she thought herself overqualified. To get the kind of job she did back home she has to pass her exam, the one proving that her graduate degree and work experience are as good as the ones you get in Canada. She's paid half her savings for tuition fees and books – binders full of photocopied sheets. It's a self-directed course that lasts eight months. In the meantime, she needs to work to pay her bills. Which is how she ends up handing out flyers.

She has to catch the morning's first bus, transfer twice, pick up her flyers, and take two more buses to get to the wealthy neighbourhood where she delivers them. The homes here are of sizes that stretch the very definition of the word "house"; they are nearly as large as some of the apartment buildings across from her, only they look more like the White House. They even have the white pillars, some of them, and fences surrounding acres of flat land. A lot of their otherwise unmarred doors are stuck with little signs saying "No Flyers Please."

Bayarmaa has learned to keep her head down, as if she doesn't see or can't read those signs. The only people who acknowledge her existence are those chiding her for failing to heed the rule of signage.

"Can you read English?" a woman says to her.

Bayarmaa doesn't register the voice at first, lost as she is in her own thoughts, unaware that the people in these homes are capable of seeing her. But the woman repeats herself as Bayarmaa turns away, and her voice is sharp, inquisitorial but somehow not quite invasive. It is late morning and Bayarmaa is nearly finished her route.

She turns back to face the woman, who stands in the doorway sipping a cup of coffee. Bayarmaa tells her that she wrote her master's thesis in English.

"The flyer girl has a graduate degree?"

Bayarmaa nods.

The woman clicks her tongue against the roof of her mouth. "What a waste."

"It's temporary."

Bayarmaa hates explaining herself to this woman. Aren't they supposed to be equals, even if one lives in a mansion? There is nothing and everything to explain.

The woman looks over Bayarmaa's head to the horizon. "Would you like a better job?" she asks.

Bayarmaa looks over her shoulder, trying to figure out what the woman is looking at. What kind of person offers a stranger a job? Only the kind of person who wants something in return, some pound of flesh.

"I need childcare," the woman says, raising her voice and speaking slowly, enunciating for Bayarmaa. "I've been waiting on the government's Foreign Domestic Workers program forever. Frankly, I'm desperate."

Bayarmaa shakes her head. She doesn't mind children, in reasonable doses, from a safe distance, but she has avoided having them for good reason. "Are you asking me to watch your children?"

"My child," the woman says. "Olive. She's three and she's got so much creative energy." The woman espouses opinions against daycares, calling them "childcare factories," and apologizes for being forward. "I know it's sudden," she says. She wants Bayarmaa to come in and meet the girl. "You'll love her. She's very intelligent." She says Bayarmaa will need a police check and references. That will be no problem; the first thing Bayarmaa did in Canada was get her paperwork done: MSI, SIN, and getting the résumé done at the employment centre. The workers there are always willing to serve as references.

Bayarmaa hears the child's voice yelling from inside. Making some repetitive, wailing sound like she urgently needs something. Bayarmaa tilts her head slightly and asks what the job pays, preparing herself to negotiate for far more because the woman is desperate, and rich. But the woman offers Bayarmaa the impossible: free room and board. No mold. She's signed a lease with the artist who owns her basement apartment. She'll have to skip out.

"Build me this," Olive tells Bayarmaa. She points at a diagram of a Lego spaceship.

Bayarmaa smiles and says she will as soon as she finishes her breakfast. The household is vegetarian and the lack of meat makes it harder to get up in the morning. Toast is a poor motivator. She quickly spoons the wet, candied cereal into her mouth as Olive runs circles around the kitchen table making spaceship noises: engines firing up, lasers shooting.

Bayarmaa finds the Lego in Olive's toy closet. The girl's bedroom is the size of two yurts. Bayarmaa enjoys building the spaceship, like a 3-D puzzle involving hunting out the right pieces – size and shape – and layering them together. It takes some time. Olive watches intently, for short spurts in between showing Bayarmaa her somersaults, then how high she can jump, then how she can do a backward somersault if she pushes off the wall.

"Look, Olive, I've done it," Bayarmaa says.

"Are you proud?" Olive asks.

Bayarmaa nods, surprised to find she does in fact feel she has accomplished something.

"Watch this!" Olive says, grabbing a toy metal fire truck and swinging it down on the spaceship until the pieces lie scattered across the hardwood. "Are you sad, Bye-maa?"

Bayarmaa shakes her head. Sorrow, no, but she would like to grab the fire truck and avenge the fallen Lego spaceship.

"Build it again!" Olive squeals, dropping the fire truck and tearing across the room and into the hallway.

Chloe, Olive's mother, was right; Olive is energetic. Bayarmaa takes her to parks, the library, train stations, the Discovery Centre, McDonald's, anywhere to let her blow off steam while Chloe does her volunteer work. Chloe's husband owns a consulting firm and spends most of his time in Ukraine helping the government recycle.

Bayarmaa is running out of ideas. She brings Olive to the compound across from her old basement apartment. The grandmothers are out with their morning teas in thermoses, chatting and watching the children, who are having a snowball fight before school.

"Fine morning," the eldest grandmother says.

"Say hello, Olive." Olive clutches Bayarmaa's leg.

"Morning, Olive," another grandmother says.

"Want to play?" a boy about Olive's size says.

Olive shakes her head.

The boy grabs a mitten full of snow from the ground and throws it at her. It is hardly a snowball, more a loose clump that disintegrates as he throws it.

Olive wails. "I want Mommy." Over and over.

Bayarmaa scoops up the child, apologizes to the boy and grandmothers, and walks to the bus stop.

The grandmothers nod and the boy waves.

Chloe is horrified when Olive tells her what happened. "What were you thinking taking her there?"

"What's wrong with it?"

"Nothing, Bayarmaa. Nothing's wrong with it."

Olive sniffles and buries her face in Bayarmaa's leg, hiding from her mother.

Bayarmaa should let it go, but she knows Chloe's scorn is

unfair. Bayarmaa has done nothing wrong and pushes the issue, asking politely as polite can be what exactly she did wrong.

Chloe says they will discuss it later, and begins her usual complaints about the "Ladies Who Lunch," the wealthy wives of faraway husbands. She has just now returned from a meeting with them to plan a fundraiser for homeless youth. "What controversy erupts when lonely old ladies plan a fireman auction."

Bayarmaa forces herself to smile. "I can only imagine."

"Oh, I wish you could join me. You've got that Zen quality."

Bayarmaa nods and picks up Olive, carries her to bed. She is shaking. Two months she has been in this meatless home entertaining a toddler. Bayarmaa tries to keep her head down but Chloe wants conversation, companionship, whatever she doesn't get from Olive, her husband, or the Ladies Who Lunch. Bayarmaa does not feel gratitude for this form of inclusion. She feels only fatigue and despair. She needs to study her textbooks, her photocopied sheets in binders.

When Olive finally sleeps, Bayarmaa tries to study, but the text blurs. Every night it's the same. Sometimes Chloe shakes her awake from her snoring and invites her to come have a drink and girl talk. "It's too early for bed," she says. Bayarmaa can't say no. Chloe relays the headlines of the day, shaking her head and speaking as if she is a magnanimous force of goodness. "I try to do my part. So many lost souls."

"We can only each do our part," Bayarmaa says, but the irony is lost on Chloe.

She passes the familiar graffiti; the swastika is still there but the paraphrased Robert Frost lines have been spray-painted over. She tries not to think about the lurch she left Chloe in. She didn't say goodbye, simply wrote them a note and left one morning before anyone else was awake. She couldn't risk being talked into staying. Her parents' debts – she had no choice.

She has to study. Maybe Chloe will bond with Olive while she waits for another live-in. Bayarmaa knocks on the grey metallic side door and waits, squinting against the morning sun.

Dan answers wearing jogging pants and a hockey jersey. "Can I help you?" he says.

"You showed me an apartment a couple months ago."

"That one's gone. Another one's available. You want it?"

The new unit is next to the one she's seen before. It looks the same and she takes it anyway. She'll have to buy a bucket to pee in at night. She'll work it out somehow. The priority has to be studying, and she starts in on the binders as soon as she's got the futon covered with bedsheets. She's on page two when the crying starts. The light wail of an infant. And two other voices murmuring, a man and a woman. Some parents at the park use leashes on their children, she recalls.

The crying worsens by page three. Inconsolable wails. Like Olive's, but less conscious, less intent. Pained, hungry, lonesome convulsed screaming. Bayarmaa can no longer hear the adult voices. She leaves her room and knocks on the neighbours' door. The crying stops for an instant and restarts. She knocks again, waits. She will offer help, just this once. Parenting is a life sentence. She will offer a few minutes of respite, that's all. Only there is no answer. More crying. Then a hoarse male whisper. She can't make out the words. Bayarmaa knocks again and calls to them. "Hello? Need any help?" She tries the door but it is locked.

Screaming, crying, wailing, choking on sorrow. Until it finally stops.

Bayarmaa puts her hand on the door. Feeling for what, she does not know. She presses her ear to it and hears nothing.

"Okay in there?" She calls it softly, not daring to yell in case she wakes the baby. Still receiving no answer, she returns to her room, desperate to study, unable to concentrate.

In a few days the police come for the father of the baby. They question every resident about what was going on with the parents, demand to know why no one intervened on behalf of the baby. Surely the police notice the conditions of the build ing but they say nothing to Dan about that. Bayarmaa tells the police she has often heard the baby wailing and wondered if the parents were home with it, but their door was always locked. It is hard not to mention that if she cannot pass her exam, she will have to return to her parents a failure. But she manages to keep everything to herself.

REALITIES

I'm twenty-seven and committing suicide the slow way when my older cousin, Starr, finally arrives at my trailer. Starr Boutelier: world traveller extraordinaire. She grew up in the next town and to me she was always stellar, in the literal sense, something from the stars. A shooting solar eclipse.

"You got my message?" she says, sunglasses propped on her poofy black hair. One tightly braided piece, dyed red, hangs over her dark face.

"I tried to call," I say.

"Oh, I had to change my number in every new country. Fucking SIM cards. How are you, darling? You just wake up? You look tired."

I stand in the door, blocking her grand entrance – surely it would be grand – and stare at her. "I'm on acid." I aim to impress her with my daring. Acid in the early afternoon, oh my!

"You're fucking kidding me. Who does acid? I haven't done acid since 1998. Can I come in?"

I stand aside.

Her entrance is rushed. She grabs her bags, runs in, and drops them. "Where's the toilet in this thing?"

I point down the hall and she runs, pisses with the door open. I half expect her to stand up. I turn away but I can hear the flood and the flush and the faucets. It's Friday. The hit I took was my last until Monday. I wish I had more. "You know Mrs. Cunningham is a dope dealer now?"

"Mrs. Who?" she shouts over the clicking of her high heels on my hallway's plastic stick-on tiles, which are supposed to look like ceramic.

"Cunningham."

She shrugs. "Nice to see you, by the way. You, uh, filled out."

"Mrs. Cunningham, my old English teacher."

"Okay."

"I told you about her all the time when we were kids. She did literacy commercials?"

"Oh. Okay. And she sells drugs? Are you really on acid?"

"Oh, all the time." Sounding cool about it. No big deal.

She fixes her eyes on me. They're blue now. "What happened to them?" I put my finger as close to her left eye as I can get without poking it.

"Contacts." She leans away. "You're a junky, Carrie? Jeez. When in Rome, eh."

"I loved your green eyes."

She stares at me. Waits.

"You can't get addicted to LSD, Starr."

"Yet you use it all the time."

"Yeah. Like coffee. How else am I supposed to deal with this wasteland?"

"Leave."

I stare at her.

She stares back. "Does this tin can come with a bed?" she says. "I'm fucking beat."

I live in a highway-side trailer, a rundown piece-a-shit. When I walk out my door I can wander in either of two directions. One is toward the post office/grocer to interrupt Dolores during her telephone arguments with her daughter, Wendy, who tortured me all through junior high and high school. When Dolores isn't on the phone she stares at me and points out the stains on my clothes. "Looks like coffee, dear.

That one is either ketchup or pizza sauce." The other direction is to the bridge, which is a dangerous temptation and probably only high enough to cripple my fat ass if I ever did jump off it.

Mostly I stay home and watch TV on a light acid buzz. Every other Thursday, when my cheque goes in, I order pizza from Dominic up the road. For years, while Starr was away, he's been the only person I really look forward to seeing. He doesn't say much but he's got full lips. Wendy used to torture him too so I feel like we're co-survivors. We've never talked about it.

I'd look forward to seeing Darlene if it didn't involve crossing that damn bridge. Darlene is my dealer and she lives in an old house on the other side of the river. Creek really. Which makes my weekly trips there doubly depressing. I have begged Darlene to sell to me in bulk, but the cow won't do it. "If you get caught with too much you'll go to jail, sweetheart." She always says that.

Darlene is the most improbable drug dealer in Canada. She was my grade seven English teacher before she retired. Now those of us left get our shit from her, and she's full of life lessons for anyone dependent on anything. Most people think she was dealing when she was teaching, but I have personally smoked dope with the woman and I know better.

The first time I went over to her place I smelled the weed on her the moment she opened the door. "Um, Jeremy said I should come here from now on?"

"Carrie, is that you?"

I squinted at her, couldn't quite place her. She had aged horribly. She was already old when I was in grade seven but then she was broad, chesty and powerful. With each step she sprung up like she was approaching the high bar. We all liked watching her chest bounce, boys and girls. And her smile was white.

Now she was wispy. Teeth gone. Face like some near-catatonic mental patient had been working it over with a sewing needle for a decade.

"It's Carrie all right. Is that Mrs. Cunningham?"

"Call me Darlene, sweetie. Come on in."

The house was a small one-and-a-half level, old and filled with antiques: oil lamps, China dolls, ceramic vases and a pump organ, little glass paperweights buckling bookshelves.

"Nice place. Darlene."

"Carrie Slaunwhite as I live and breathe. I thought you'd be saving the world in Toronto or something at this point in your life."

"Mm-hm."

I get this a surprising lot considering I don't go out. My mother says the same thing, in less friendly terms, every month. She peers up at me from her open Bible, her stomach rumbling and a sardine-smelling burp seeping from her slightly parted lips. "You're lazy like your father was till I threw him out," she says. "Too lazy to get a job here or anyplace else. You should branch out." I've been getting that from her forever.

And the whole town crawls with former teachers, all of them surprised I never went anywhere. Most of my classmates did, down to the States or out west to work. No one around here is hiring. Barely any businesses left. But this is my home. More importantly, Mom still needs me to hear her complain. Somebody's got to. I'd feel worse if I left her. Better depressed here than guilty in some big city where no one has time to notice all your success anyway.

"So is it true you sell drugs now, Darlene?" It was fun saying her first name, drawing out the second syllable to make it leeen.

She smiled. "You were one of the good girls, Carrie. Not just well behaved but ... creative. Not afraid to express your ideas."

I looked at her, hating this. Hating that she didn't remember what I remembered. That is: the year after I had her as my English teacher the other girls let me know what they thought of my ideas. The same girls I'd once bounced with on a neighbour's trampoline decided I had too much to say and was monopolizing all the conversations talking about my dreams of flying around the world someday. They didn't offer any specific alternatives to speaking my mind; they merely humiliated me every time I opened my mouth. It was easy for them. I was scrawny then, smart but eager to please. The only reason I'd been so talkative was to impress them. I didn't know what the girls would do to me if I stood up to them; I just knew things would get worse. At my house, failure to please resulted in pain.

No boy ever snapped my bra at school – the girls beat them to it. They stole my underwear as I was changing for gym, wedgied me with my jogging pants, and called me camel toe. Then it got worse. They took photos of me naked in the locker room and posted them on the bulletin board with the caption, "Carrie the Crotch." The nickname stuck tighter than the wedgie.

What good did expressing my ideas ever do me?

But those girls are long gone now. So is my one good friend, Jeremy, the soft drug dealer. He got a job in the tar sands. You got to wonder about a job that pays more than selling illegal drugs. Regardless, those jobs have been good enough to take away everyone decent from our town.

"How did an English teacher get into selling dope?" I asked Darlene.

"Have a seat, Carrie." She pointed to an antique wooden rocker in pristine condition. "Dope, as you call it ..." she pulled a rolled joint and lighter from her tan cargo pants and lit up, took a drag, and passed it to me.

It's not my drug of choice, but I accepted out of deference to the teacher.

"It's my only relief from pain. I'm dying, Carrie. So when sweet young Jeremy left, he introduced me to his supplier and now I get all I need wholesale. And, contrary to previous plans, I can keep my house. It's good to have an income again."

"But what if you get caught?"

She smiled again, all gums. "I wake up every morning and greet death. What do I have to be afraid of?" She reached over, plucked the joint from my fingers, and took a drag. "Anyway, who'd suspect a sweet little old lady like me?"

Darlene's okay but I hate going there, crossing that bridge. So I buy ten hits at a time, once a week. It's all she'll sell me, like I need another mother at this point in my life. One is more than enough. There are a few other dealers around but they're farther away and I don't much feel like developing new relationships if I can help it.

I limit myself to two hits a day, Monday to Friday for a nice steady, light high. But it leaves a little too much reality on the weekend. Better that than Monday. On the weekend at least the news is slow, and they throw in a lot of those "lighter side" stories. Notice they don't promise anything funny, just light, relatively speaking. But even on the weekend the news is the news: more wars, the Earth getting deep fried, murders and car crashes, more unemployed losers like me every day. Saturdays are long, Sundays I've got football to watch, and Monday mornings I'm back to Darlene's.

The walk to her house is purposeful; it flies by. On the way back I stop at the bridge, look down at the ripples in the water, each one a Fundy tide on my brain screaming for relief. "Boring!" I shout, not sure what I mean, but thinking about how much better I'd look in the air, wearing a pilot's uniform, the shoulders ruffled slightly for the sake of femininity, my hair cut shoulder length and arcing out from under my flat cap with visor. In this fantasy the hat has golden wings etched into the black brim, and a golden bar going around the base. It's so hot, as are the half-naked men I relax with on foreign beaches between flights, their skin darker than mine and muscles bigger than Van Damme in the *Bloodsport* movie. My fantasy goes a little off the rails from there – like everything in my life – but the part about flying a plane, being able to look down at those several dozen gauges and switches and being in total control, banking the wings to slice acute azure skies, I've dreamed of this since I saw *Flight of the Navigator* as a little girl. The movie was about a spaceship, not a plane, but at the time I thought the flight scenes over major cities and oceans had changed my life. This was before the bullying and before Mom turned from absent-minded to drunk and cruel.

In my weakest moments, or maybe my strongest ones, I think about becoming some other kind of professional who doesn't have to travel so much. Maybe a family doctor: set up shop above the post office so Dolores can finally stop bitching about having to drive all the way to Halifax every time her acid reflux acts up. But I'd still have to go away for school. These are my silly dreams. They beat reality. And acid beats my silly dreams.

Looking down at the water, my heart is racing, anticipating. I take a hit. One is enough to start. Ease into it.

I take another. I breathe deep. Look at the water. It's less boring now. It's laughing at me, like chattering teeth.

The river laughing reminds me of Wendy, after she convinced me to take a post-gym class shower. I can still see her half-smile, the cartoonishly suggestive arch in her left eyebrow. "The other girls are too polite to say it but I want to help you, Carrie. And, well, how can I say this? Um, like, you smell a tiny bit ripe. And people are noticing." She giggled and let her face stretch into a full smile, oversized teeth gleaming. She was like her father, who owned a car lot just out of town, and who once told me he could "sell air conditioning to Eskimos." Only Wendy could tell you that you stank and have it sound like she was your best friend. Sure enough I had my doubts, but voicing them seemed more dangerous than complying. She said she'd lend me a towel. But there was no towel and when I came out of the shower my clothes were gone. There was Stacey Reed, standing in the middle of the locker room with her dad's Polaroid flashing. By the end of the day I was dubbed "Carrie the Crotch."

Even my mom chuckled, at first, when I told her about the incident and the nickname. "Oh, Carrie, you idiot. How could you fall for such an obvious trick? Grow a pair, would you?" Sipping her rum coffee as if I didn't know what was in it. Me knowing she was about to completely lose her shit, my teeth chattering like they came from some novelty store.

"Least I don't need alcohol to make me tough," I mumbled.

Now the river laughs at me, all grown up standing on the bridge again, thinking about jumping. The river knows I won't. Isn't this humiliating? But a laughing river is at least a little more interesting than one that trickles lamely through a highway town half-full of losers – the other half having left already.

I go home to watch the midday news. The mayor stutters like Elmer Fudd, rationalizing his crackdown on wascally wabbits. "Don't you er uh people know how wascally dey awe?"

And then my world-travelling cousin, Starr Boutelier, makes her grand entrance.

Starr spends all of ten minutes in the bedroom, which I am surrendering for the duration of her stay, a timeline she has not made specific. She flies out of the bedroom the same way she flew into the trailer, only without the full bladder. She's got on a teal chiffon gown, sleeveless. So homecoming.

I'm in the living room watching *The Young and the Restless*.

Starr tackles me, splays me across the couch and pins my shoulders, presses her nose to mine and looks me in the eyes. Her green eyes are back. I think for a second she'll kiss me, which is scary but would be an interesting if disgusting break from the routine. But she doesn't kiss me.

"I missed you, Cuz," she says. "You know? So. Fuck it. Got any beer in this place?"

"Can't afford it. Acid's cheaper."

"Is Key Largos still open?"

"Yeah. It's called Florida's now though."

"My treat." She calls a cab and I have a shower. When I come out she's watching Y&R, crying.

"You okay, Starr?"

She looks up at me, swipes at her eyes with the back of her hand, and nods. "Can I ask a question?"

"Is it about acid?"

She takes in a heavy breath. "Do you keep your mother's skeleton in your bedroom closet?" She's turned sideways on the couch, facing me, but her eyes are focused on the ceiling. She's shivering, arms folded.

"Dude, my mother lives two miles down the road. Why do you think I stay in this place?" I stay in this place so I can visit the old hag once a month and appease my guilt listening to her bitch about everybody else in town, complaining that all the church committees are falling apart now that the other old biddies have kicked her out and told her to get help with the drinking problem, the one she swears she doesn't have. At some point the alcohol's going to finally kill her and I want to be nearby so I can rush to her and say I told you so. Only problem is I haven't yet worked up the guts to tell her so.

"Oh," Starr says. "Okay. Thanks. But ... can you bring my bags out of your bedroom for me? So I can get changed?"

I nod and turn away, go to the bedroom, and I have this burning in my gut, same as I had when Wendy helped me get my training bra off for that fateful shower. How was I so gullible? But this is Starr. Starr was never a bully. Judgmental, bossy, full of herself, sure. But she'd always looked out for me. I throw on jeans and a T-shirt and drag her bag to the living room. Starr's on the floor now, between the couch and the coffee table, looking up at the ceiling with her fingers in her mouth, shivering.

"What is it?"

"Fucking spiders, Carrie. Your tin can is infested with spiders."

I look up. I want to see spiders. I want to see what she sees. I wish I had more acid so I could join her on her trip. But there's nothing there except the mildew. I squeeze in with her, moving the table to make room for my bulge, and hold her head, stroke her hair like when we were girls. I pick her phone out of her pocket, call and cancel the cab. They don't come half the time anyway.

On Monday I tell Darlene about Starr, who has bought a tent and pitched it behind the trailer because I insist on storing my mother's skeleton in the bedroom, and the rest of the place has a spider problem. She says she'll be moving to a motel this evening. Apparently there are also hairless cats infesting my backyard.

Darlene mumbles something and I retrieve her teeth from the jar in her bathroom. Her speech is getting worse. "Schizo-phrenia," she says. "When's the last time you saw her?"

"At her graduation. She's been living in India and Nepal and Bhutan since then." After her first postcard from Bhutan I had trouble finding it on the world map hanging at the post office.

"Often schizophrenia doesn't manifest until the early twenties, or later. You need to get her help." She hands me my stamps. "Want to share a joint? On the house. Help you calm down."

"I'm calm."

"You've practically worn a hole in your pants."

I look down and see the threadbare fabric on my thighs where I've been rubbing away with my thumbs for three days. Old habit. Wendy used to call me Thumb-hole-ina, when she wasn't calling me Carrie the Crotch. I accept the joint, take a toke, and exhale. "I got to go, Darlene. Thanks for the advice."

She smiles, flattered. "Nice to be of use before I die."

"Don't talk like that."

"Why not? It's reality."

"Exactly."

She surprises me with a hug. "Don't forget my offer," she says.

She wants me to take over for her when she dies. Promises me she'll leave me the house and everything. She never married or had children. The free house makes it a tempting offer and, despite whatever promises she forces me to make, I'd be able to do as much acid as I want without leaving the house every week. And I'd be doing something useful. The whole pilot thing seems less likely every year. But becoming the local dealer? Moving to a new house? It's a big change. I don't like change. "I'm thinking on it," I say.

Darlene smiles. She's taken her teeth back out and her face looks crumpled.

I smile and leave, walk to the bridge, take four hits and a deep breath. What a waste what a waste. It'll be a long week with only six hits left. Breathe, look down. White knuckles, gripping the railing, leaning far forward.

Only one time did I challenge my mother about her drinking, too many years ago. It was right after the shower incident. I muttered it underneath my breath, accused her of drinking to feel tough.

Before I hit puberty it was Dad who drank, and hit her and all that bullshit some men do to their wives when they can't find work. And she took it and took it and took it until

I guess one day she decided, in a short minute while he went to take a piss, that if she chugged down his rum he wouldn't be able to get any drunker and he wouldn't hit her so much. Then, drunk off her own arse, she got all this courage and started giving him shit, saying he made too many excuses and he gave up too easily when he couldn't find a job in town. "You need to branch out." Gave him a sweeping backhand to the shoulder when she said "branch out." He was so shocked he didn't hit her back.

I guess she liked that courage because she kept on drinking. He did the same. Sometimes the two of them got drunk together and insulted and hit each other. She'd call the cops and they'd send Simon Peter, some kind of distant cousin of my dad's and a long-serving friendly neighbourhood policeman. You can imagine whose side Simon took, but having the squad car show up in the driveway all the time had to be humiliating. That's what I figure, given that Dad left after only a few months of this. I can't quite remember what he was like, other than drunk and frustrated.

We never heard from him again, but Mom kept drinking and all her liquid courage got channelled my way. It wasn't as bad as what Dad used to do to her, but it was bad enough. She'd shove me or slap me or tell me I was adopted and that adopting me was the biggest mistake of her life. And when I told her, the one time, that she only thought she was tough because of the booze, she went for her white Bible, the *Good News* version. It was the start of a great ritual that we enacted several times a year until I moved out.

She had me clutch the back of a chair and brought the Bible down on my knuckles. Crack. On white knuckles. Again and again. And her white teeth, not chattering but sneering. "How could you be so stupid, falling for such an obvious lie?" Chastising me because Wendy bullied me. Crack. "Or maybe you are an exhibitionist. Maybe you wanted what you got. Unrepentant slut." Crack. "My bad luck to adopt an idiot

slut. Must get it from your biological mother." Crack. White
door opening, my mother pointing to a tiny closet. "Take your
clothes off and get inside. Idiot. Exhibitionist slut."
    My white legs shuffling, red blood seeping from white
knuckles.
    Then a click. Darkness and her god-like voice from be-
yond the door yet smothering the room. "Thou shalt beat him
with the rod," she chanted, "and shalt deliver his soul from
hell." I suspected though that she used the Bible only because
it was the heaviest book we owned.
    After that I kept quiet about pretty much everything. But
silence didn't save me from anything.

    I stop at the bridge on the way home and stare at the
water. Everything has gotten confusing since Jeremy left. Too
much change, like some new bully is shuffling all my carefully
arranged cards. And now Starr. The weird things she sees. I
don't know how to handle that. Maybe I can send her to live
with Mom and they can be insane together.
    I don't know whether to accept Darlene's offer. It's a step
up from nothing I suppose. But it also means I'll never be a
pilot. Never get out of here, never stop listening to Mom complain. I can't think about all that now. I have to find a way to
help Starr.
    "Boring!" I shout down to the trickling water. I stick my
fingers down my throat, puke over the bridge, and watch it hit
the water, yellow fizzing to light purple. Would my blood look
that cool if I jumped?
    A van stops right beside me. I stare at it and shake my
head, trying to get it to focus. It's jumping like an old TV with
a bad connection. The van is teal, the same color as Starr's chiffon gown. But the side of the van has a photo of a very cheesy
piece of pizza being pulled away from the rest of its pie by a
hand, and the hand is attached to an arm. The arm is covered
with little spiders.

Dominic, who owns the pizza joint and makes the deliveries too, climbs out of the van. His chest hair dances over his collar, do-si-doing with a sparkling gold chain.

"Everything okay?" His moustache looks lonely, without a dance partner.

"Fine, Dominic. Fine." I force a smile. I'm still clutching the railing, but leaning back away from the water.

"You sure?"

I wipe a dribble of puke from my chin and grab the railing again. "Yes. Okay now. Thanks."

"Okay." He gets back in the van and drives away. Dominic never says much. I usually like that. Right now I want him to stay and insist he can see that something is wrong, that something is always wrong with me. I want him to really know me. I don't expect him to help. I just want him to get it. It's so obvious he cares.

I look after him, after the van spitting fumes from the back. The flesh is gone from the picture of the bare arm attached to the hand holding the pizza on the side of the van. The arm is just bones now, a skeletal arm with spiders on it. I wonder where the hairless cats are.

I shake my head, trying to clear it. Schizophrenia. Crazy. Things like that aren't supposed to happen to Starr. She's Starr. She's completely in control of all things at all times. When she used to visit me, back when we were kids, my dad would get sober for the weekend. Later, Mom did the same. When Starr visited, Wendy left me alone. Starr had charming magic or intimidating voodoo, something that made everything around her okay. Now she's freaking over spiders and hairless cats and the skeleton of her aunt, my mother, who is alive and whole-bodied and drunk down the road. Starr's reality remains much more interesting than mine. But it's completely out of her control, not like before. So horrifying and evil.

I fumble the rest of the acid as I pull it from my pocket, drop all six hits to the water. The little stamps flutter and land separately, not heavy enough to make a splash, barely a ripple. Damn, what a waste.

Happy, Starr? I bet she is. She who always had control and now supposedly has none. I wouldn't be surprised if it was her magic or voodoo that made me drop the acid into the water, a big "fuck you" to her new reality, that is, her new loss of reality, the one she never asked for, that forced its way into her brain. Regardless, I can tell her I quit acid, for now. She'll like that. And I can tell her about Dominic, how he stopped to check on me.

STAY LOOSE

The lights are flashing, the bell dinging, and Dad drives his rental car straight through, over the railroad tracks, a split second before the bar starts descending. My four-year-old son, Jacob, waves at us from the backseat of Dad's rental, looking serious.

I jab my foot at the gas pedal, determined to keep pace, but the bar has gone too low and I brake hard to a stop. The train whistle haunts my ears. I watch as Dad keeps driving, oblivious to the fact we're stuck on the other side of the tracks, Mom and I in front; my husband Allan, our seven-year-old son, Kenny, and the dog, Muffler, in back. We're on an ill-advised road trip, driving south to the border and into Maine, the first of four states we'll visit, culminating in a game at Fenway.

The train is forever long. As we stare at the passing train cars, Mom counts off a long list of my father's flaws, her voice soft and scratchy but steady with no sign of relenting. Every word drives my fingernails deeper into the steering wheel. When I was a little girl, we bonded by complaining about Daddy, but at some point I let the game go and she kept playing. She hasn't yet gotten to the way he coddles his grandchildren and can't even change a diaper or plan a meal.

Jacob insisted on going in his grandfather's car. Dad was pleased. Now he's alone with a four-year old who could panic if he glances back again and sees an infinite train instead of me waving. He's a clingy kid. I like him that way.

The train brakes to a stop. The car behind us honks and I stick my head out the window, which is rolled down because the A/C ran out of Freon last summer and we never got around to having it refilled. I yell to the round-faced woman behind us: "It stopped!" I'm just passing along some intel but her face reddens and she starts yelling back at me.

"Listen to the mouth on her." I say this for Allan's sake. When I made the list of reasons for and against marrying Allan, his steady-as-rain amusement with whatever chaos the world throws at him was number one on the pro side.

"She's a foul-mouthed woman, Grace," Mom informs me.

I can't actually make out a word the woman says.

"Cover your ears, Kenny." Mom makes a show of putting her hands over her ears, her bulbous knuckles looking ready to pop, her fingers bent and twisting in different directions. It's a wonder she still embroiders.

I turn off the car. Allan reaches from the back, turns the key a click, and puts the radio on, flipping through stations.

"You're going to kill the battery," Mom says.

Allan mumbles something about "updates."

From my Con List: Allan shuts down around my mother, hides his most boisterous booming self from her vigilant cynicism, and leaves me to fight her alone. I want him to join me in battle. At first I admired Allan's ability to hide himself from her, go completely unnoticed so that we managed to get engaged and set a wedding date before my mother ever commented on him one way or another. Finally she said he was smart. Subtext: not particularly handy around the house.

Pro: Allan is stealthy like a le Carré character. That's hot.

Mom affects him too though. He's quieter about it, sure, but he grinds his teeth and shortens his syllables, blunting the consonants for maximum impact. But for her presence he wouldn't be shushing Kenny, who wants to listen to the baseball broadcast. Allan barks at our seven-year-old boy and

Kenny barks back, and Muffler actually barks and the three of them glare at one another like drunks in a bar while Mom looks on approvingly because Allan is being strict and she thinks that is good parenting. Whatever they're barking it's monosyllabic and of the three, Muffer's voice is the clearest, least slurred.

"Enough!" I stare them down, daring them to defy me. From the top of my sightline I catch a glimpse of the red-faced woman in the car behind. Is she still yelling at me? I think she must have seen me yelling at the boys and assumed it was for her and yelled back. She's opening her car door. "Fuck me."

"Grace!"

"Sorry, Mom."

"Apologize to your children."

"Jacob's not here," Kenny reminds her.

"We should call George," Allan says.

"His phone is off, Allan. By the way, that woman is coming here to punch my face."

"He must have turned it on when he realized we were stuck behind the train. What woman?"

"He doesn't even know how to turn his phone on. Also, the woman behind us – beside us – is going to punch me."

I turn to the woman and greet her, reassure her I wasn't yelling at her, only the stupid males in the backseat of my car.

The woman, when seen close up, is about a half-foot shorter than me and not as fat as I'd thought. I can't understand what she's yelling – she's speaking Ukrainian, which happens to be my mother's first language. Mom has a knack for finding other Ukrainians wherever she goes. Mom yells back at her, her voice breaking at the strain of her volume, and the two women are yelling and pointing across me. I lean forward to protect Mom but she pushes me back with a hand and keeps shouting. She's laughing as she shouts. The other woman, who is about my age, is laughing too.

"What the hell is going on?" Kenny says.

"Language, Kenny."

Muffler barks.

The woman pulls something metallic from her back pocket and for a split second, as the sun glints off it and into my eye, I think she's shot a gun at us. But it's a flask. She takes a sip and hands it to my mother. I reach for it and my finger glances off it as it crosses in front of me. Mom takes a shaky gulp, some of it dribbling down her chin, then hands it back to Allan, who raises the flask to Mom and the shouty woman and takes a gulp, as if they're old war buddies. "Thanks, Julia."

"Thanks, Julia," I say in a dumb-male voice. Best of frigging chums, they are, when the booze comes out. He's a goddamn enabler.

"I'm thirsty too," Kenny says.

A uniformed man approaches us from the front of the train, walking with his head down and his eyes on the track, seemingly oblivious to the growing line of cars held up by the train. He must be the conductor. He's got the hat.

"How's she going?" He stands next to the Ukrainian woman and addresses his comments to me. "Just to let you know what's happening, we had to put her into emergency. By Christ I got to walk three kilometres or so, so's I can be sure where the break is."

Mom and I question the conductor but his rural twang is almost nonsensical and I worry he may be drunk, wonder if I should call in and report him. I never thought of myself as someone who reports people. But really, if the train is broken down shouldn't the police be on the scene, directing traffic or something? The conductor says the only alternate route would be the main highway, which takes about an hour of backtracking to reach. I glare at Allan.

Pro: adventurous, spontaneous.

The moment the conductor moves past us the flask is back out, coming from Allan back to Mom, who takes a swig. I reach for it and she bats my hand away. "You're driving."

I know she's dying for me to ask her about the Ukrainian woman but I won't give her the satisfaction. I need to get out of this car. I go for a walk back down along the road. There are a dozen or so cars behind us. I tell each driver that the conductor says it'll be at least an hour. Most of them turn around. Probably locals.

If Allan has a list about me, are some of the pros my take-charge leadership, my willingness to help out, my commitment to unbroken communications?

In planning this trip, there were challenges with Allan, Mister Spontaneous, the anti-planner.

"Should we camp or motel? Dad really wants to camp."

"Your mother would rather sleep on the roof. Maybe we can pitch a tent for your dad outside our motel room."

"No tent then."

"Glad that's settled." As if making this decision had been a grave burden on his soul. As if he couldn't believe he had to deign to put an iota of his great intellect toward figuring out this trivia. I wasn't without sympathy when the maps came out because I knew he had the spatial intelligence of a stationary bike.

He'd never admit it. He'd rather wave a hand at my boring maps and say, "Stay loose! Because, you know, control is an illusion when you think of it. There are too many powerful forces in this universe beyond our control."

The "stay loose" aphorism comes from a favourite anecdote of his, a friend who was heli-skiing in the Rockies and, surprise surprise, fell down a cliff. Miraculously she survived and when interviewed afterward told the reporter she had to keep reminding her body to stay loose, to surrender control to the mountain and hope for the best because if she fought the mountain, she would die. The first time Allan told me that story I was in awe that he had a friend like that, so bold, brave, and wise, and rich enough that she could hire a helicopter to help her seek thrills. Later, I saw a similar story posted on Facebook and got a little suspicious, but it didn't matter. By then I'd grown to hate this friend of Allan's who I'd never met, for her privilege and new-age bullshit.

Look, if I ever fall down a mountain I'll remember not to have a plan.

Even with two cars we hadn't been able to fit everything in. Allan made the executive decision to leave the cooler behind. We'd have so much fun eating at truck stops along the way. That was the way to discover the real America. And my mother, who when sober prepared every meal I ever ate as a child, right up to my graduation dinner, went along with it. "Allan is the boss."

Allan had nodded as if he were comfortable with that role, as if Mom had the power to assign it to him, as if her hands patting her pockets down like she was checking for cash weren't a dead giveaway to how nervous she was thinking about eating in a truck stop. I shuddered to imagine her giving some greasy waitress her money to prepare inferior meals and coffee.

We've eaten all the apples and crackers and drunk most of the water we brought. We decide to leave the heat of the car and spread a beach blanket on the grass beside the road. While Allan and I do the blanket, Mom goes back to invite the other Ukrainian woman to join us; Kenny tags along to get his harmonica. Mom and the other woman are still shouting at each other in Ukrainian when they come back with a fresh bottle of booze. Allan shouts occasional random Ukrainian phrases he's picked up to amuse Mom. They reward him each time with bellowing laughter.

I know Mom wants me to ask what they're talking about but I won't. The three of them are getting shit-faced and Kenny and I are getting irritable. I try Dad's phone again but it's still off. Allan gives me an annoyingly calm look that says everything will be fine and I growl at him. Kenny whines for the hundredth time that he's bored and I snap at him, more mad at Dad, Allan, my mom, myself. Kenny's not supposed to be responsible yet. He's the only innocent here besides Muffler. "Where is Muffler?"

"In the car," Kenny says.

"We cracked the windows, right?"

"Actually," Kenny says in the professorial tone inherited from his father, "I put them all the way down just to be sure." He stares at me, his face expecting I'm not sure what, praise or laughter or maybe a scolding for being snide.

I look to Allan, who is already on his way to the car at a jog. He stumbles crossing the ditch and gets up dusty but doesn't bother to brush himself off. We all watch, the first silence in hours, waiting as he opens the door and sticks his head way down as if to look under the driver's seat. His movements drunkenly exaggerated. He looks back and shakes his head.

"Gone."

Mom belts out a staccato laugh.

I glare at her as we walk back along the tracks. She ignores me but she has to feel the blame. She was with Kenny when he went to the car. She didn't tell him the windows were down too far, that the dog could get out. It didn't occur to her to bring the dog back with them to our little picnic. She was more concerned with a stranger who happened to speak Ukrainian. She can't ignore my glare forever. If I have to smack that bottle from her hands she will acknowledge what she did.

"Mom!"

She pretends to look underneath the train for the dog. Let's be clear about Muffler: he ain't going to win Smartest in Show any time soon, but he's not dumb enough to hang out under a train. Mom's as drunk as Allan and thinks she's fooling me. She's good at hiding it but I hear how she slows her speech and movement just enough to keep control of it. She looks brighter when she drinks, or less pale anyway. Her hands are steady as she leans on a train wheel for support so she can peek down really low.

"Mom!"

"I thought I heard it bark."

"*He.* Muffler is a boy."

Mom shouts something back but all I hear is "dog" because her head is mostly behind a train wheel. She's pretending to look around underneath. The woman will risk decapitation to avoid talking to me.

I start to tell her off but my words and thoughts get jumbled and I have to turn away, close my eyes to the sun directly above us, glaring. I mean to ask her why she is the way she is, why she is so angry at my father for his every shortcoming, yet it's her who laughs when a beloved pet goes missing, and she only pretends to help us find him. These questions are nonsensical, useless accusations. Aside from a few moments of childhood cuddling, she has always been an a-maternal entity, an expert planner and preparer of food, more maid and life organizer than mother. Asking her why is like asking why the rain falls.

I want to challenge her for this one thing, this lost dog. I sit down in the bright heat on the grass by the train. "It's your fault." Mom doesn't answer, and I sense she's moved farther up the track.

I open my eyes and see her ahead, not that far, and I chase her down.

"Muffler!" Kenny shouts, not a plaintive come-here-boy but a thrilled there-you-are-boy. Perhaps I have overestimated the big mutt's intelligence. Muffler isn't under the train but rather on it, atop a flatbed car gnawing at a dead pigeon, some of its feathers fluttering from his mouth. He's always been a masterful pigeon hunter, cat-like in his stealth, quick enough to snatch them before they get airborne.

The train jolts forward an inch and Muffler jumps down into Kenny's arms. It's not a big jump but it's enough to knock

Kenny to the ground. Muffler is panting to the point of froth-ing. Mom tries to give him a lick from the flask and I slap her hand away.

"It was just a joke."

"Frigging hilarious."

She pouts like I'm the bully.

We realize the train is really moving now and run back to the car, waving goodbye to the Ukrainian woman. Running proves a waste of energy because we still have a minute-or-two wait before the train has passed.

The rental car is not on the other side of the tracks and Mom starts ranting again, saying Dad's probably driven with Jacob halfway to Maine without noticing we weren't behind him. "Or stopped at a casino."

We find him at the far end of a long line of cars, standing next to the rental with a big smile on his face, holding Jacob with one arm and a Big Stop bag in the other.

"Well, hello there," he says when we pull over and get out.

Jacob starts handing out burgers and pops like a Red Cross worker at a disaster zone. I hate it when Kenny pours a bit of cola into Muffler's mouth but I know the dog is parched so I let it go, stay loose.

"We were rather famished. We couldn't wait, could we, Jake?"

Jacob tears into my arms. I wrap them tight around him and let him sob into my breast. I need to comfort him as badly as he needs my comfort. "Jakey, you come ride with Mummy and Daddy. Grandma and Grandpa will go in their car."

I turn my back on my mother and walk to the car, deafen-ing myself to her protests.

ARSONISTS

Today I am ending the life of my grandmother, who raised me, whose life force was incendiary. She burned off the poison my parents instilled in me early, which otherwise would have killed me.

I am joined at Grandma's deathbed by my life partner, Ana. Our two little boys are at Ana's mother's house. Ana has been my rock since Grandma asked us to put an end to her pain. I couldn't do it without Ana's steady reminders that this is what Grandma wants, that she wouldn't have put such a burden on us if the pain weren't crushing her. So why do I feel alone in this task?

Ana and Grandma, they're close. But Grandma knew me when I was ten, determined to be Patti Smith, and forgot to bring my punk-rocker costume to the class Halloween party. At the time, Grandma was a receptionist for a lumber company owned by the richest family in our town. My school was named after their patriarch, a self-superior man who insisted his employees arrive twenty minutes early and leave twenty minutes late with no extra pay, because "maintaining a professional work ethic" was his own secret to success. When I called Grandma crying about the costume, she told Mr. Barston she'd be taking an hour for an essential errand and would pay him back with two hours of her time the following week. She may as well have been Jesus on the water showing up in the principal's office with my half-shredded Sid & Nancy T-shirt, plastic slitted shades, and spray-on hair dye. She had saved my rock-and-roll career.

Grandma loved me long before punk had occurred to me, when I was going to be a veterinarian. She piggybacked me all around the zoo and explained the fecal processes of the charismatic mega-fauna we saw. She was already in her sixties. Once when my own fecal process failed, she explained the workings of the suppository to distract me as she inserted it then cleansed the consequences when it worked oh so quickly.

I've shared these memories and many others with Ana. Yet their weight is mine alone as I travel the roadmap of lines criss-crossing the skin around Grandma's blue eyes, which lead her head side to side, still instructing me, now that her voice has failed. Their weight is mine alone as I inhale the scent of Grandma's hair, of smoke from the decades of fires she tended late into the night and again before anyone else had woken. She loved chopping wood and stoking the stove. Their weight is mine alone as I steel my resolve.

You promised her, Ana says in her scattershot movement in and out of the big green-walled room, around the queen-sized deathbed, fussing over irrelevant neatness as Grandma sleeps. *When every breath hurts, what's the point?*

I'm not sure that Grandma's pain is exactly what Ana thinks it is. It's true that her breathing is grotesquely laboured, each inhalation a wheeze and a whimper so awful the children wince. When Grandma could still speak, she said little frayed wires were pricking at her lungs. A while ago we reached the point where the only sufficient dosage of painkiller was that which knocked her unconscious. But there's a deeper layer of agony; she is weighted by her own memories.

When I was in university she started talking to me about the little girls. *My gut burns knowing I can't tell them it's not their fault.* At first I thought she was speaking confusedly about me. She'd said as much when I was a kid, that the pain I was going through – multiple surgeries removing tiny shards of glass from my head – wasn't my fault. That I shouldn't blame myself for my mother's demon temper. But Grandma was speaking of something that had happened before I was born. Only after a while did her random sentences make some sense. Something about little girls being forced to eat their own vomit. But why? At whose hand?

The same autumn Grandma saved me from my mother's drunken chaos, the old Indian residential school burned to the ground. It was down the road from us about a mile, halfway between our town and the reserve. The building went up like a firecracker in the night and all the natives came down from the reserve to watch the smoky ghosts rise from the charred bricks. That's the impression I was left with from our chatter, for we all came too, from the town, and stood in our own group, no one traversing the invisible line between them and us. Although none of us from the town were native, there were experts among us, as there are experts on everything in any gathering. *This was once their burial ground*, one man said. I watched Grandma's face for a reaction but her mouth was closed and her lips were flat, her eyes only reflections of the dancing firelight.

I once taught here, she said, quietly and just for me. *Not long before it closed. They must be happy to see it burn.*

Her hand was slippery as she walked me toward the group of natives. She stopped a few paces away and I noticed another old woman holding another little girl's hand; she was a few years younger than me. The old woman was crying. I called out to the girl that it was going to be okay. I imagined that I was her big sister. Her glare dried out all the love I'd felt for her. I tried to forget the hurt of that stare, the perceived betrayal, and a faint scent of fuel distracted me from it. I asked Grandma if they hated us. She said they mainly hated our church. *Our priests and nuns.*

Years later, when I was in university and Grandma started talking about the little girls, it took me a long time to connect the trail of her thoughts back to what she'd said that day watching the suspicious burning of the old residential school. She'd already developed a tendency for rambling and she started speaking of fancy spoons and knives, her mother's insistence on the proper placement of endless utensils for formal functions, the importance of cleanliness. I finally understood what she meant when she said, *I didn't care about rich people's functions; I wanted to help the needy, to get my hands dirty. I certainly did that.*

I tell Grandma she has lived an honourable life and done more good than harm, ask her to let go whatever guilt she feels. For a while her eyes ignite with something, then wander as she whimpers, as if looking for an exit. I could sob with her every murmur. Instead I medicate her unconscious and still she moans in her sleep. It burns me too, not knowing if she understands me when I speak. I need to do this deed, whatever the consequences for myself. In my shoes, would Grandma worry about herself or the person in pain?

Ana encourages me but she often follows me into the room to watch how I interact with Grandma, a protective layer against merciful death. Ana is afraid of consequences. Sometimes she leaves us alone and goes to visit the boys, who have been staying with her mother these final days. Ana calls me and complains about them, what a handful they are without me around. *They sense weakness.* She's not a weak woman, but a bit too serious for those miniature clowns.

A mercy kill is surely harder than giving birth. With childbirth, once the process begins you can scream all you want, drug yourself and curse everyone you've ever loved, but the thing is still going to happen and then you have to cut the cord. I can't simply inject a needle and set myself on a course of loss, cut away the woman who has sensed the intent of every twitch of my skin, known distant thoughts before they began their marathon toward my mind, confronted phantom memories of violence or defeat and massaged them into nothing more than fatigue.

I climb into the bed with her and stroke the thin white wisps of her hair. I fall asleep to the rhythm of the movement of my hands on her scalp. I dream that we are firefighters attacking a burning building full of sizzling, popping pieces of pottery made by small hands. I smell gas and realize I've lost sight of Grandma. I panic and whip my leaden fire hose around. It has become intolerably hot, burning my hands. I drop it when I see her off in the distance, lighting a rag inside a rum bottle and hurling it through a window in a brick wall. The whole wall shatters then explodes.

The kids, back from their other grandmother's house, wake Grandma and me in the morning, snuggling in with us, taking unusual care. But Grandma is whimpering again. The time has come. On our command the boys kiss her goodbye like it's a race; they don't know the plan. Ana tries to take a moment but Grandma coughs blood. Ana takes the kids to the park. Grandma may go naturally now, I think, but her soft cries are too much. I inhale deeply and fetch the needle from the sink. It's been sterilizing, not that any foreign bodies could be worse than the main contents. I wish we could do this in the house where Grandma raised me, where she set out our meals, mine a version of hers with crusts or anchovies or spices removed. But a new family has long since torn it down and replaced it.

Grandma's veins, once well hidden beneath pale skin, are now an angry, throbbing purple and easy to find. I try to maintain eye contact, uselessly hoping for one last moment of connection, but I need to focus on the vein. I end up kneeling on her chest to get the right angle but it slips through her thinned skin easily enough. When I lie next to her, her eyes finally stop searching. I rub her hair again, so thin over her bumpy head, and the breathing slows, quiets.

I think about that burning school building and wonder, as I often do, if Grandma was kind to the children like she was to me, and hope again that she was not one of the cruel teachers they talk about.

The fire was arson. Someone torched the place. I like to think that someone could have been Grandma.

TAKE HIM TO A BETTER PLACE

Coach Henden is going to take a puck to the face. All the parents of the B-level kids agree it's coming; it's a favourite topic of conversation as we wait for our bitter canteen coffee before our little Hornets in their "gold" (yellow) jerseys stumble onto the ice for the first period. We've got a pool on which of the kids on Henden's Triple-A team will be the culprit and how many months into the season it'll happen. I say Rogan Flieger before the end of January; he's got the hardest and most accurate wrist shot any of us has seen on a twelve-year-old. I saw him moping in the parking lot one time, hours after his practice had finished, when my son Kevin and I arrived at the rink for Kevin's practice. When I asked Rogan where his mom was he pushed past me, leaving a trail of little-boy musk and fury. But he lives right down the road so I figured he'd be all right making his own way home. He isn't a bad kid, just competitive. Fiery, Coach Henden called him, "like myself."

If Henden is a bearish presence, sucking back lunchmeat sandwiches packed by his never-seen wife and spewing crumbs as he shouts orders at the kids (who look deceptively like men atop their blades slicing between cones on the freshly Zambonied ice), Rogan is an alpha cub learning the art of the roar, how to intimidate with size and speed for the sake of an abstract yet pinpoint focus, snapping hard little round black discs past heavily padded goalies and across six-foot red lines. He is a favourite of Coach's and the recipient of his loudest orders.

"Take him to a better place!" He shouts it whenever he wants more aggression against the boards. The kids are technically a year away from being allowed full-body contact.

We're all bad people for partaking in this ritual, hockey in general, and hockey gossip especially. I'm the one who organized the pool, created a Google calendar with the name of each kid on Coach Henden's team and a check box next to it, all over a watermark image of a fat guy with a bloody forehead. Look, you can only take this kind of humiliation in life for so long. Forty-four years is enough for me. Finally I go to the Henden residence and his son, Oliver, answers the door, chewing a sandwich, crumbs falling from his mouth as he tells me his father can't talk right now. Oliver is a tall, slight boy with wavy golden locks, more retriever than bear, and it's the first time I notice any resemblance. "Just tell him to check his goddamn e-mail, or answer a text!" I sputter, feeling the two shots of whisky I steeled my nerves with more acutely than expected as they mix with an adrenaline rush. I want to high stick that kid.

That night I e-mail him for the ninth and last time and I'm long past sparing details of the advantages given my competitors when I tried out for Triple A in 1989. I was the last kid cut and Dad still whispers to his friends, in the same reverent tones he uses when recounting the first time he heard the Rolling Stones, about the beauty of watching my long hair flow back from under my helmet, such was my speed and grace. But he wasn't part of the local hockey royalty and he let my mother take me to practices; unlike the other parents, she lacked the good sense to get to know the coaches and make my case for me. These are things my father says matter-of-factly and I embody my father in my final e-mail, begging Coach Henden to give Kevin a chance, which he does in fact answer: "Decisions already made if ever short goalie will text."

When the text comes I've just cut my lip shaving. I have blood on my teeth and soaked into four pieces of tissue in blotchy polka dots. I jam a fifth against it and hold it tight with one hand, check my phone with the other.

"Can he practise tonight? 7:00. Stephen has mild concussion."

The phone whistles again. "Empire rink."

An hour from now. I've promised to take Adria door to door selling chocolates for Girl Guides. Kevin has to study for a math test. He's excited for it. The teacher says he has a shot at repping the school in Toledo, Ohio, at the Math Olympics. Ohio. Jeanine has a board meeting; she joined the board of the Riverkeepers now that the kids are older and a little more independent. She left me detailed instructions on how to heat up and assemble the components of a moussaka she mostly prepared this morning, before sunup. "You got to learn to roll with it." Jeanine's advice on surviving parenthood. I'd taken the same approach to childhood, enduring my father.

I answer Coach Henden. "He'll be there." We'll do Girl Guide cookies another night.

The practice is a prelude to a weeknight game. The added events in our schedule require more shuffling, new spreadsheets from Jeanine. She's the schedule master. The game in turn is a prelude to a weekend tournament in Dedmon. I'm nauseated, half from fear and half from way too much drive-thru.

Kevin looks bad in practice. He's replacing an older, longer, quicker kid, Steve, who took a half-full coffee thermos, no lid, to the head. He is not only mildly concussed but also mildly burned on the cheek. The stainless steel missile was aimed at the ref. Steve had only flipped his mask up for a quick drink after allowing a power play goal. The parent who threw it is banned from the rink and is lucky Steve's parents didn't press charges. They shared the other guy's outrage at the ref. In Steve's stead, Kevin faces breakaways, two-on-one drills, and slapshots. "Henden pushing him to see if he'll break," I text

Jeanine. My phone whistles response after response in rapid
succession. I can only squeeze and shake the thing. I know it
sympathizes with my contempt for Henden, but I'm fixated on
Kevin's every save attempt.

When the horn sounds, Kevin out-skates them all to hus-
tle off the ice, showing unusual speed for a goaltender. He
stares me down in the dressing room. No one speaks to him,
though the boys shout at and over each other, bragging about
top-shelf shots and blue-line cannons, arguing about best NHL
teams and players. Some of the cubs roll and wrestle, growl-
ing and biting playfully on the floor. Henden thanks Kevin for
coming out.

"It's too hard!" Kevin says in the car, his voice hiccup-
ping. "Those kids, they shoot and it's impossible to save. And
when you do it hurts. They aim where it hurts. And they can
hit their spots."

"You made some nice saves."

My phone whistles. Jeanine again. Her previous messages
are all links to articles on the hyper-competition we subject
boys to and the sociological weapons they become as a result.
The last one a question: "How'd he do?"

Sixteen boys naked from the waist up, billowing black
hockey pants below, long wool socks and under-armour sneak-
ers all in a pileup, screeching at varied inharmonious pitches
wailing playfully on one another. The sun on the backs at the
top of the pile. One boy smiling silently off to the side, T-shirt
on, sitting on his goalie pads and chewing at a hangnail, his
sandwich unwrapped at his feet. After a 4-3 loss in Kevin's
first Triple-A game, they've managed a 7-3 win in the first
tournament game. Henden ordered them to relax until their
next game in three hours. "No swimming at the hotel. Eat a
nice light lunch with chocolate milk and fruit. We're playing
Greatville tonight and they beat the guys we just played 12-0.
A shutout."

But Coach isn't here now. He's at tomorrow's opponents' game. Scouting.

Other parents are nervous about the pileup. Some say my boy is so well behaved and others warn their sons of the danger, until one mother sees a limb sticking out and hauls her boy loose. Somehow the rest of the pile stays intact, fifteen boys left. I'm nervous about Kevin, how he's handling all this. I whisper encouragement, that he should join the fray. "Jump on, dude, you can be at the top, king of the castle."

He emits a high groan, shakes his head. "Rogan said it was my fault we didn't get a shutout."

Kevin got his first glimpse of hockey at Madison Square Garden on his fourth birthday. He had zero interest in any of the junk I bought him. Not for him the day-glo orange nacho cheese or salt-butter popcorn or jumbo pop or hotdog. The lights of the rink lit up against the ice, the pageantry of the anthem, the team lineups, that was what he ate, his face alive and eyes wide, scanning his horizon and missing nothing. He fell in love with the uniformity and order of it, six identically dressed men dancing on blades, knowing where all the others were and would be at all times, so the body beat the puck to the spot though the puck was faster. And at the end of every shot the goalie's pad or mesh or leather. It was a 1-0 game and the man with the most elaborate equipment won the day and first star of the game.

At home Kevin tied a couple of Jeanine's novels around his shins with my neckties, paisley and plain black. His chest protector an apron. On his head he wore Jeanine's bike helmet and a colander as a mask, taped on with masking tape. I shot a rubber ball at him in the kitchen as Jeanine circled around making spaghetti, draining the noodles from the pot with an undersized lid while Adria shouted out random addition problems.

Kevin didn't save a thing, not even the soft knucklers;

even the little rollers along the floor squeaked between his legs, five hole. I've never seen him happier.

The bloody face is mine. Coach Henden's face is still fat and flawless.

I was right about one thing. Rogan Flieger fired the puck. It was my fault. I was leaning in from behind the net, not expecting the kid to shoot yet, telling Kevin to move out, challenge the shooter. His reaction time wasn't quick enough to stop the bullets these kids were firing so he had to give them less space, force them to be more accurate. The word "accurate" was in my mouth when Rogan let a shot go that just missed the glove side, top shelf, and ended my first session as an assistant coach.

Henden had asked me to fill in for Andy, the regular goalie's dad. I'd told him so much about my minor league career, he figured I was qualified enough to sub in for a last-minute practice. He'd learned no one had the ice booked for the hour preceding our game and he jumped at the chance to work out a few bugs. "Give Kevin the protection he needs. Get the kids in a defense-first frame of thinking."

Rogan was never supposed to get any kind of decent shot off anyway. The drill was all about taking away angles. The defense let us down.

We're all prisoners to the destiny these boys make manifest in forty-five minutes of game time. Even the coaches can only yell instructions from the bench – half of which are lost in the cavernous echo of last century's hockey architecture – or play with the lines a little. Kevin has no backup.

The rest of us, me with fresh stitches and a wad of super-absorbent surgical fabric – blue soaked in red – stuffed in my mouth, can only shout our encouragement to the boys, our disgust at the antics of the opposing boys, our criticism of the teenaged referees, all of which is lost to the ancient rafters under a din of cowbells and air horns. We've been warned, no more objects to be thrown on the ice.

After the second period, the Zamboni run prolongs our agony. Due to the gauze in my mouth I can't even soothe mine with shit coffee. The Greatville Miners score another two in the third. It's not quite a blowout and the moms say, "Kevin held his own in there" and "He made some good saves" and "Kept us in the game for a while." The dads don't look at me. I'm about to make an excuse to go to the car when Henden invites me into the room to join the players-and-coaches-only meeting, because I had that fifteen minutes as an assistant coach.

I follow him in, dodging and hurdling boys wrestling on the floor with their equipment and each other, and find Kevin in the corner, still fully geared up, skates, pads, chest protector, and mask. I put my forehead against his and search out his eyes. Forlorn or scared, I can't tell. "Good game." But through my swollen lips it sounds like "Goo gah," and he bursts into an all-too-brief fit of laughter before poising himself.

Henden bellows orders for everyone to sit down and shut the hell up. The kids snap into reverent silence, backs against concrete. Eyes on Coach. The assistant coaches do the same and I follow their lead.

"How'd we do?" Henden says.

"Bad bad-baad." Their voices almost synched.

"Be specific. What did we learn?"

One by one, starting with Rogan, the boys go around the room. "I wish I'd backchecked harder."

"We weren't careful with the puck. Except Jonas. He did a good job."

"Thanks."

"It's true."

"Yeah, you were our best player."

"We didn't protect Kevin enough."

"Our offense was good."

"Yeah, we took advantage of our opportunities."

"Jonas was player of the game."

"But also Kevin."

"Kevin?"

"Yeah, Kevin made a couple big saves."

On it goes, fifteen boys with specific observations. Kevin in silence. But at least, when Oliver nominates him for player of the game, he takes his helmet and mask off.

Coach Henden raises his hand and they stop. "Player of the game is Kevin. You can't play without a goalie."

The kids and assistant coaches dutifully clap. I pat Kevin on the back. He smiles at the floor but it's meant for me, an inside joke I don't get.

"So obviously we learned our lessons today. I expect we'll kill Saint Gordon tomorrow."

The numbers aren't right. I can't focus. The facial wound has affected my brain. No, my phone is stubbornly focused on an impossible time.

"Kevin. What are you doing up at five a.m.?"

"Cops." He's peering out the motel picture window, holding back a stained mauve curtain with his blocker hand.

He jumps back when I approach, like he's sliding across the crease, as if I'm winding up to shoot. I give him a quizzical look.

"You look like garbage, Dad." He points at my face.

I rub the dry blood caked in my stubble, overnight leakage from my mouth. I pull back the curtain again and see a local police cruiser, lights off, and two uniformed officers chatting with Henden. The discussion is animated, at least on Henden's side of it. Hands gesticulating wildly. His forehead glistens under the parking lot lights. Could be sweat or the light snowfall.

The cops are calm, hands open at their hips, a professional position surely picked up in basic training or whatever the Mounties do. If it were a yoga pose it'd be called "I'm listening." One of them nods and the other gives a little smile, the kind enablers give assholes who say hateful things.

Henden sees me, waves me out. I put my hand to my chest and shrug, a cartoon gesture. "Who, *moi?*"

"Go, Dad. See what he wants."

When Coach calls …

The air outside is frigid. My ears tingle with it the moment I open the door. They are stinging by the time I reach Henden and zip up my coat, nodding to the officers but with my eyes locked on Henden's.

"You look like shit," he says.

"What happened to you?" an officer asks.

Before I can answer the officer, Henden tells me what's going on. "Little incident with the wife back home and they call these local guys to get in touch with me here. Since cops don't know how to deal with mental illness I got to head back." He glances sideways at Exhibits A and B, then reaches out to me. For an awkward split second I think he's going to hug me. I brace myself for it. He clasps my hand, squeezes it like a vice, and shakes it to pulp. "You can take the bench today. Rob's certified. Johnny knows the lines. You, you get them to say good things about the weakest player. Otherwise they'll turn on him like fuckin' hyenas."

He holds onto my hand, eyes locked with mine like a championship staring match. I start to stutter my condolences about his situation, his wife, when he lets my hand go and struts to his car. The officers chuckle, doff their caps, shuffle to their cruiser with me trying to come up with some smartass remark.

Henden rolls by slow, his passenger-side window down, and I notice for the first time that his tall skinny son, Oliver, is sitting in the backseat, waving stoically to Kevin in our motel window. I catch Henden's voice in the air, trailing off as he accelerates, "… good as your weakest guy."

Yep. Only as good as your weakest player. The coaching clichés haven't changed since 1989. And who might that be, I wonder, strolling back toward my son, hand on my face finding fresh blood.

HOW FAR BEYOND ME SHE HAS GONE

When Candy told me our daughter had been assaulted, I thought I'd lost her.

"Her ex-boyfriend, I think he drugged her," Candy said. It took a moment to register the underlying pain and anger. I'd been gazing out our picture window, absorbed in the orange light of sunset cutting through the branches in silhouette.

I stumbled rising from my easy chair. I couldn't traverse the distance from the living room to the stairway leading to the basement, which we'd recently renovated into Ada's apartment. My feet were mired in a sticky synapse someone spilled all over the hallway. The floor was electric with it. It jolted my nerve endings. I lay down and shouted Ada's name from the floor.

"Ada!"

"Yes? I'm alive!"

I hadn't considered the alternative, or that her fate could have been even worse. I pulled myself up, ran downstairs, needing to see whatever was left of her.

She sat cross-legged on the floor with a schoolbook in her lap, looking whole – blue jeans and plaid shirt open over grey T-shirt, reading glasses on above half a smile. "Yes, Father?"

"Tell me what happened."

She went silent and empty.

"Did it really happen?" As they left my mouth, the words protested they were the worst possible choice.

Ada responded with a yowl that froze me to the stairs. I stumbled over clichés and quotations, frantic for something worth saying, something to give her. Whatever words might have eased her pain eluded me.

Candy appeared, tugging at my sleeve, rescuing me, giving me permission to run. I became vacant light. Candy led me to bed. I lay there, more in love and more frightened than I'd been at Ada's birth, when a nurse handed her to me, her slime-encrusted scalp resting in the crook of my elbow, her eyes closed but her middle finger raised in a harbinger act of defiance. The nurse said, "Oh, you got a little rebel on your hands, Daddy."

I hadn't wanted children so much as I'd wanted to make Candy happy. Candy later talked about how everyone says you're supposed to experience love at first sight with your kids, but she didn't. I did. It hit me in the stomach like an all-encompassing muscle cramp; the pain of it brought song to my throat: "Tea for Two." I didn't think about the meaning of the song, or why it was written for Doris Day, or that determined look of happiness in her eye. I just sang and smirked at Ada's tiny middle finger flipping me off, taking care not to drop her, or otherwise shatter the spell.

This violation of Ada, her tattooed skin and hard-beating insides, felt like a massive epidural administered by Fortune. It froze me to my bed. I told myself, "This isn't about you," yet there I remained, helpless. Candy always says I have to learn to let go of that which I cannot control. A father is not so reasonable. He will work himself to death to create alternate realities for his daughter and fill them with every meticulous detail she desires, an overpriced frilly dress, a junior high soccer team's trip to Big Beaver, Saskatchewan, a tattoo based on Grandma's lacework, engine-mechanics classes. There is little he won't agree to, work toward, pay for.

Nothing I could buy for her now.

From the earliest, it seemed a particular challenge to keep Ada alive. She crawled early, walked early, sought electrical sockets early, swung from our porch railing over our concrete patio before she had the arm strength or coordination to properly throw a ball. By grade school, she was climbing almost to the tops of eighty-foot oaks on our suburban streets every time I turned my back. Keeping her from danger was a full-time job.

Candy had promotions to earn and I had nature documentaries to write, shoot, and cut. I took only a week off work after her birth but I agreed to take the night shift tending baby. That is, if Candy's milk didn't put her to sleep, I would rock Ada's sorrows back to blackness. I confess, in the delirium of darkness, I begrudged the baby, felt an impulse to let go as I rocked her, imagined releasing her at the apex of the back-and-forth swing. I tried to be perfect, to absorb each word of her stream-of-consciousness descriptions of every blessed moment of her school days, meanwhile longing for one of those quiet kids who gave their parents monosyllabic answers when asked about school. Worse was my nagging, unspoken sense of resentment when puberty arrived and she and her mother engaged in closed-door conversations about training bras or feminine-hygiene products.

I have put the entirety of my heart into this girl. When Candy loses her temper with Ada's attraction to trouble, I encourage them to stop shouting and hug each other. Yet Ada's fallback emotion with me has often been anger. When I bought her a stuffy for her thirteenth birthday, she let me have it, shouting that she wasn't a kid anymore. It was the first-not-last time she told me to fuck myself. I couldn't decide whether to let it go, because it was her birthday, or take away her phone, her connection to everything. I settled in the middle, let her rant and storm away, and later reminded her of better ways to express frustrations.

"To be honest, I hate that you hate the bear. I guess you're growing up." I thought I meant it.

Subsequent occasions when Ada dropped an F-Bomb on me: while throwing her purse in my face because I told her to be home by 10:00; while storming out and slamming the door when I said she should be careful with the boys she was dating, harmless as they seemed, because they wanted only one thing, or some daddish banality. I should have gone after her. I was afraid I'd lack the strength for any more descriptive insults she might articulate.

Once, when she was quite young, Ada told me she was "not very pretty." Boys loved to play with her but they never had crushes on her. I told her she and her mother were the most beautiful girls in the world. "I know you think that," she said.

Lately, she has become something more, in terms of her looks. Attractive. Those little boys, who used to love having water-gun fights with her, look at her in a new – fuck, I just need to say it. They desire her. They want to touch her. They want to run their gangly teenage bodies over hers. She surely longs for the same. I'm aware of this on the rare occasions we embrace, on birthdays, Father's Days. During less common spontaneous moments when we long to show we love and are loved, and the embrace is mangled by the terrible feeling of her curvature, the knowledge that she too must be aware of her impending adulthood, and is repelled by it. Yet we both need to matriculate the procedure, the scarce ceremony of showing mutual affection.

When Candy told me what happened to Ada – that one of these teenaged boys touched her and more against her will – and when she guided me into bed, I chastised myself for this entire line of thought. Why was I being so self-absorbed, when I should have been consoling my daughter? Should have been reminding her there is good in the world and that she was not at fault? I could have been hunting for evidence against her ex. I could have been at the boy's house and – that's how one father in small-town Illinois handled it, the dude who made the news after his daughter's basketball coach was convicted of molesting her. The father attacked the coach in the courtroom. I'm not sure why he waited until then. Maybe he needed the judge's confirmation of the coach's guilt. I was already certain of Ada's ex's guilt.

In the days that followed, I let my wife take Ada to the hospital, the police station, a counsellor. I let Candy take our daughter to all the places that might have helped her heal or move on. Where they could discuss the fact that this boy Ada cared about – who collected knives and had delineated for me his passion for one knife in particular, a butterfly knife he liked to twirl around his fingers and flip in the air, "doing tricks" – pinned Ada by her shoulders to the vinyl backseat of his Ford Escort and forced up her skirt with his knee.

I wanted and did not want to be there with Ada and Candy. It was the feminine-hygiene products all over again, a rattrap of facts that are biological and straightforward but simply don't apply to me. The possible answers to my questions – Was there blood? Did he have one of his knives with him? Did he threaten worse? Did he threaten people you love? Do you have nightmares about it? – terrified me. Instead of asking, I listened at night as Candy told me about rape kits, paperwork, and tears. I nodded, was thankful that although Candy didn't love Ada at first sight, she grew attached quickly and they are close.

I took on more than my usual share of housework and cooked all the meals using organic vegetables from the market. Ada's a vegetarian. I don't know what I expected when I presented them with mushroom bruschetta, or chestnut, spinach, and blue cheese en croûte, but Ada hardly touched any of it, just swirled her fork through it in circles like she did when she was little, her lips flat and her hair over her eyes. One night I blurted out a casual "What's wrong?" desperately hoping for detail on some other more minor thing that we could talk about, a more easily surmountable problem. She snorted and rolled her eyes.

When Candy and I went to bed, I confessed to feeling awkward around Ada. Candy told me a story that I'd told her several times, about when I was in early adolescence, thirteen or fourteen, and I tried to punch a man who had whistled at my mother on the street. I missed so badly I spun in a circle and fell to my knees. When I got up, the man tousled my hair, winked at my mother, said, "Brave kid" and walked away. My mother told me she could handle herself.

I told Candy I must have been in one of the stages of grief. "Denial maybe?"

"Just a little behind the victim then."

I told her about my friend Felix, who made jokes about his twenty-year-old son deriving pleasure from intimidating his sixteen-year-old daughter's suitors, looming over them with endless rhetorical questions: "What do you want from her, exactly? Huh? Why you hanging around with her?" Why is that funny, I'd wondered at the time. I wished Ada had an older brother, or that I'd been the kind to take pleasure in scaring young men. All the boys Ada brought by seemed like children, capable of no more than toilet papering our house at Halloween, barely able to maintain eye contact while making the most rudimentary of small talk, answering softball questions with grunts. Had I properly interrogated them, they may have shit their pants in my kitchen. My daughter is larger and has more kinetic energy in her pimples than any of them have in their entire skins.

"Sounds like you're in the bargaining stage," Candy told me.

I talked for a while about other friends of ours, Dolores and Tristan, who spent seven years adopting a baby boy they named Clay. When Clay was two years old, doctors diagnosed him with neuroblastoma, cancer of the nerve tissues, after Dolores took him to the hospital due to fever and constipation. Dolores, an insurance lawyer, quit her job to manage all the tests and treatments – the radiation and transplants. Tristan fell apart, tagged along to appointments for a few weeks then said he couldn't take any more time off work. They split up over it and every time anyone mentioned Clay or Dolores to Tristan, he went silent, as if hypnotized by some internal fixed point. If you mentioned Tristan to Dolores, she vented for hours about all she and Clay had been through without support. They'd sold the house. She hates insurance now, calls it "an industry of gluttony, greed, and wrath." Tristan took a job in Boston. A few months later Clay was in full remission. He still had to have monthly checkups. It was still all Dolores talked about. She'd lost many friends. "Fake friends," she said. Clay doesn't even remember the chemo.

Candy listened, although she knew the whole story herself and probably wondered what my point was. I couldn't bring myself to say that in the end Clay's cancer was harder on his parents than it was on him. Not that Ada's assault was harder on me than it was on her. It was just that Clay was oblivious to having been sick. I barely recognized Ada in the girl moping around my house. I was powerless to undo what had inflicted her.

If Candy caught the drift of that, she didn't say so. She rubbed my chest. "You need to talk to your daughter."

I agreed to take Ada to a scheduled appointment at the police station. In the car, she played the radio too loudly to talk, a song by a young man imploring a young woman that he could treat her better than her current beau could. She deserved someone like the singer. At the police station, I wanted to escape, as if I were guilty of something. I glanced around. Behind us were two exits. Beyond the desks in front of us, down the hall, I saw what looked to be the corner of a jail cell. A police officer introduced himself as a member of the sexual assault investigative team. He had thin, blonde hair atop a square head, high cheekbones, and static eyes peering from behind square glasses. There was nothing on the desk but an open laptop and a mug with the Golden Gate Bridge on it.

The officer spoke in a monotone about statistics. He constantly used the phrase "sexual assault." Rates of sexual assault are high here, he said, highest at the beginning and end of the school year. "The latter of which is approaching as you know." He told us how many students there are here, university and high school, and that they make up most of the victims, most of them drinking and/or drugged. The sexual assault report rate is miniscule, he said, so law enforcement believes the real sexual assault rate is significantly higher than the reported sexual assault rate. "For girls, we recommend the buddy system."

"Come on every buddy grab another buddy's hand?" I stared at the officer's gun, hanging in its holster over the side of his wheeled office chair.

"I mean travelling in female groups."

"Like the Spice Girls."

He coughed into his hand. "I mean never accepting a drink from a stranger. Making sure to cover their drinks. Never leave a drink unattended." He did not say Ada should have dressed more conservatively. Neither did he accuse her of perfuming the air with sex. He also said nothing about the choices of the young man.

"You getting this, Ada?"

"I just came to get my dress back."

I repeated her words to the officer because, although I understood her, she was slouched down, forehead in her hands, speaking to the floor.

"The dress is evidence," the officer said. "DNA."

Ada didn't move. She was as stoic as the officer. I asked more questions. I do the interviews for my films so I'm comfortable asking questions at least. I asked about the DNA, whether it was necessary given everyone knew exactly who drugged Ada. Instead of answering the question, the officer talked about the drug the perp used. He reviewed Ada's symptoms: the rash, the nausea and blurred vision, the severe hangover despite having had only two drinks. "All consistent with ketamine, a common date-rape drug."

"So with the DNA we can get this kid convicted, right?" Here the statistics compounded. The officer reiterated the miniscule report rate, noted the miniature report-charge rate, the wee charge-conviction rate, and the near-perfect probability Ada's every behavior – her tattoos, her once lying about her age on a waiver form so she could go skydiving without our permission, her underage drinking, her history with this boy, with any other boys, school suspensions – would be revealed, scrutinized, and leaked to the media, given her father's modest local fame for his minor involvement with a movie that was once shown on American television. "You have to go in with your eyes open and be ready for the worst."

Ada erupted from her chair, sending it tumbling back. She bolted to the exit.

I struggled through the process of breathing, trying to be more conscious about it, which Candy says is useful in high-stress situations. I had to follow Ada, but first I tried to catch humanity in the officer's eyes. "You got kids?"

He nodded. "Little boy."

I waved him goodbye, not saying anything more about DNA or Ada's black dress, which I thought was too short and too old for her when Candy bought it.

I thought about the officer a few days later when I read a news story saying eight women had reported being attacked and violated at that year's Mardi Gras in New Orleans. It took me back to my own visit to Bourbon Street's student-tourist feeding frenzy, throwing beads up at two cheerleaders on a balcony, my friends and I thinking we were men, shouting, "Show your tits!" If you got your beads over one of their heads, they'd oblige and rub their naked breasts together. One of the women in the news story said her attacker was a security guard and that it happened next to the police station. The youngest "woman" was eleven; the oldest was sixty-three.

I told Candy the bright side is things are always worse somewhere else.

"Some bright side," she said.

"Listen." I tried several times to frame my latest thoughts for her, managing only to babble. "I should talk with her more. Open the lines, like, maybe we take a trip."

"I can't right now. Work is too –"

"No. Just me and her."

I could have shared hundreds of good memories with Candy about our daughter. Ada and I binging on ice cream, fries, and *SpongeBob SquarePants* while Candy worked through long weekends. Me helping Ada clean her room until she found a lost remote-controlled truck. Her windmilling her arms and spinning to Katy Perry at her youngest aunt's wedding, her arms and legs flailing yet the whole of her body coordinated, power pulsing through her movements, her raw athleticism already on display. Her first airplane flight, her staring at the seatbelt light with fingers hovering over the clip to remove it the moment the light went off. I especially loved musical memories: singing her to sleep at night, well into her teens, with "Tea for Two" and her serenading us each morning from the shower with a belted and slightly off-key rendition of "Zip-a-Dee-Doo-Dah."

Although the synthesizing act of remembering these things charged me, like when I first heard her heartbeat through the ultrasound, I had to admit that lately I had not put my whole heart into this girl. This young woman. I'd resigned myself to her departure for university in a few months, making the power struggles no longer seem worth it. My laziness was reflected in her every eye roll. After all my anxiety about the lust of hormonal boys, and the possibility of reciprocation from my equally but differently hormonal girl, the reality that one of them had forced himself on her unwilling body was far worse. That he'd invited Ada out that night for old times' sake, to a party at his cousin's house in the sticks. That he'd pulled onto the cracked asphalt of our driveway, honked his horn as she ran out the door with a tossed "See yah," that he'd whipped around the potholes on our cul-de-sac in his little old beige Escort, her forcing a giggle as she swung around the front seat still struggling with her seatbelt. That he'd made her mixed drinks with an illegal drug in them, a drug he'd probably bought from some other kid at school, that paralyzed her muscles and numbed her skin, so that her mind would be present but – creating a near-death experience – her body would be powerless to stop him. All those times I had stood at the bottom of a tree she was climbing, ready to catch her if she fell, and this was how the world hurt her.

This line of thinking, this was how I found myself outside the young man's house in my own shitty little car, at midnight. I came to observe, a mission of reconnaissance. I didn't feel anger toward him, just perplexity. I needed to see his face again, to reconsider it. Maybe I'd understand the world facing my daughter when she left our home sanctuary. His house – his parents' house – filled its whole lot, leaving enough room for a six-foot-square patch of grass and an off-white concrete driveway, which had a little '90s-model sports car in it, a Miata I think. No sign of the Escort. The place was standard suburban, very new, pale yellow with white trim and flower boxes under the windowsills.

From the other side of the street I was almost invisible; the house opposite was small and dark, no sign of life other than a child's bike lying near the sidewalk. I sat outside the silence of Ada's ex's childhood home. I took in the stillness of the unpainted porch and wondered what each channel of vinyl siding said about the boy. Did he ever disappoint his parents by drawing on the exterior? Carve his initials into it with one of his knives? Were they amazed when he grew so tall he bumped his head on the flower boxes? Before the Escort, did his father let him borrow his prized Miata? I hadn't given him much thought until then; I'd been thinking about Ada, how far beyond me she had gone.

The front door opened and he stepped onto the porch. The space between my fists was the wreckage of a collapsing stellar core and I smelled charred flesh. I hadn't moved so easily past the anger stage as I'd thought. I wanted to crush him like a stale orange. I could too. The boy was even less than I remembered. He was shorter than Ada, had a plain round face and straight-cut mop of light-brown hair, partially covered by a red cotton hood, nothing like the latest pop-chart hero. He had a determined gait as he headed out on foot.

My seatbelt was coming unbuckled before I felt my hands moving. I could almost feel his fragile body under me, hear the crunching of his bones as I put my weight into him, threw my fist into the cartilage of his nose, turned my face from the spurting red. Breathe, I told myself. Like Candy showed me. For high-stress situations. In. Hold. Out. Eyes closed.

I sat, feeling oversized, like a basketball player in a clown car, breathing slowly, thinking about Ada. The time she wanted a regulation soccer net in the backyard. Candy didn't want to sacrifice the lawn. Ada was dominating her Under-12 league and I felt she deserved support. I could have bought a prefab backyard soccer goal, regulation sized, but the ones online looked flimsy despite costing hundreds of dollars. I took inspiration from some YouTube kid who made a goal out of sheet wood and a tarp. Ada laughed at the kid's video, how he stumbled on words and said noncommittal things like, "I had this idea, I don't know why, but I just wanted to do it." But she was full of ideas for how we could improve the basic concept and use better quality materials. Her teammate's father let us use his toolshed and helped with cutting and planing the wood.

Ada and I worked on it for several weekends, first a version where I lashed the posts to the crossbar and frame, like we used to do with lean-tos in Boy Scouts. It was strong enough but Ada said it looked a little too *Trailer Park Boys*. We undid it and drilled in long screws. Everything about it was perfect; the sun rose and set at angles that never put it in the keeper's eyes. For as long as Ada used the net, as long as she invited me to take shots or make saves, I happily cut the grass twice a week. Until then it had been my least favourite chore. I remembered that, smiling, clutching the inside door handle of my car, slowly relaxing my fingers. But I was still angry driving home. I ran downstairs to Ada's apartment and found her sitting cross-legged on the floor, texting.

"Maybe I should just fuck him right up!"

She looked at me as if she'd never heard such language in her life. Yet she responded in kind, throwing the same word back at me, wondering what the exact fuck I was screaming about, and why?

"Your ex."

Her expression shifted from confusion to exasperation and she told me I was out of my mind. "He's nothing." Her voice cracked and she tossed her glasses onto the floor. She covered her eyes.

I wanted to confess where I'd been. What I'd been doing. To show her, at least, that I cared enough to do something. Although I hadn't.

Ada made a noise, a high stabbing whine. It accused me of becoming part of the violence against her. It reeled in any truths I might otherwise have spoken.

"Ada, I was – I just … I wanted to help you get it back."

The noise stopped but she kept her hands over her eyes. "Well, Father. You can't."

I reached down for her hand, to help a fallen teammate up. She pulled me down instead, which was better. We sat together for a long silence, breathing together.

"Look," she said. On her phone, she showed me the dress she wanted to buy for prom. "I co-chose this hot little number with my date." She flipped to her photos and showed me another round-faced floppy-haired boy. Jake. Or Josh. J-something. The dress was pink, a colour she hadn't worn since grade one. It had a bow in the middle, frills at the bottom, which

Ada said she wanted to twirl so she could hear the swooshing sound. "Swoosh," she said, smiling, making her hand move like an ocean wave.

In the picture, on the thin, blonde model with painted ruby lips, more makeup than I would ever let Ada wear, the pink swooshing dress was a good five inches above the knee and still showed a healthy top-third of the model's exceptionally healthy breasts. The breasts were the only healthy-looking thing in the picture. Like a Barbie, her legs were about ready to snap at the knees. The model was, as you'd expect, beautiful. In the face, breasts, hips, thighs. Ada, I knew, was beautiful too, but nothing like that. She had pimples. Her legs were thick and strong. She was tall yet had a low centre of gravity, a powerful core anchored in muscular glutes. It made it impossible for opposing strikers to get by her. She had hair on her arms, like her mother. Like human beings do. What do models do with their arm hairs? I wasn't sure about this dress but that wasn't my main concern. It was the J-boy she "co-chose" it with, that potential killer.

I couldn't lecture. It would only shut her down. I wanted to keep her talking. I asked about the dress, prom, her plans for the summer and beyond. She told me she was applying for transition-year programs. She had no idea what she wanted to be. She planned to start a summer coaching clinic for Under-14 girls. "That's when most of them quit."

Was she that courageous, that she could simply move on with her life? Or was she acting out some mechanical response to trauma? Was she fearless in the way only a child unaware of consequences can be? Like when she used to fall off her bike, wash streaks of mud from her face with tears, scoff at my suggestion we take a break, hop back on and go again. She was no longer that determined little scrape-kneed rascal with an underdeveloped amygdala, yet she still blazed through life as if she was without scars.

"You could take a gap year," I said. "I wish I had. Never did hitch to Mexico."

"You and Mom would go crazy if I hitched around."

"I could go with you."

"Come on."

"For a bit. Get you started, fly home by myself after a week or two. Get away from all this stuff."

"Never come back."

"Reinvent ourselves. Start over someplace else, with new identities."

She snorted as if she had abandoned such fantasies back in her childhood days. "Father," she said. "Don't you know? No matter how far you go, you can't escape yourself."

SHIMMER, SINNER SINGER

Shimmer is a word I equate with beauty. Shimmery tide. Shimmering light reflected, refracted, oscillating like music – visual reverberation. Like a bare bulb reflected in a glass of shiraz. Shimmer and desire. I was always desirous of topaz dresses hugging muscular frames, the juxtaposition, yin and yang and effeminate macho.

This road-tarring work I was doing (middle-aged and I had to go back and take a course before my cousin, who'd always taken pity on me when we were boys, hooked me up with his old friend's crew), it related. But it was also a rusty nail slowly puncturing a lung. It paid okay. It was hot work and the shimmer, though sexy, was of the sun and fresh asphalt, a lesson in how tar splatters up into pant legs or onto my abdomen, sizzling flesh and body hair. Pain was inevitable, and carried a stench of hopeless repetition.

I needed a shovelling mantra. Numbers might be good. Something rhythmic. Hip hop. I remembered a youth camp. One of the kids wanted to do this song for the talent show and we had to crush his aspirations. "You can't use that language. It is cruel to certain of God's children. God does not play favourites, you see, and he does not condone bullying with words."

"But, Pastor, this song is by Black guys. Black guys are allowed to say it."

"No one says it here."

I slammed my shovel through the shimmering sunlight and felt afire, sun all over my shirtless torso, muscles straining, repeating, seeking oxygen, finding more pain. I tried the lyric, or, that is, the numeric, non-offensive part.

"One. Two. Three and to the four. Snoop Doggie Dogg and Dr. Dre is at the door."

Again. Mantra. Non-religious mantra. God hadn't forgotten me but I wished He would.

"One. Two. Three and to the ..."

No. That wasn't me.

This wasn't me.

I looked at the other men, knowing nothing of their worlds beyond our work together and their meaningless banter, their skin bright red in the first scorcher of the season. All headed for blisters. All unable to bear a rayon-polyester vest in that heat. All straining in the inferno, like me. But faster. All in their natural habitat. Not me.

It was hard to think of a non-religious mantra. At the very least it had to be reverential. "Cleansed by the shimmer. Cleansed by the shimmer."

No.

"Cleansed by the pain. Cleansed by the endorphins."

The men around me joked with one another, elbowed each other and pointed with their lips to pretty drivers in summer dresses. Hot.

"Jesus loves me this I know. For the Bible tells me so. Little ones to him belong. They are weak but he is strong."

The men laughed so hard they stopped working, leaned on their shovels, and roared from their bellies like fat cats in old gangster movies, only not fat at all.

I smiled at them, pretending to be in on the joke. They were looking at me. I was at the end of the row and the six of them – Raúl, Jon, Dave, Ken, Bunker, and Salim – had all stopped to look at me and laugh.

"Where'd that come from, Paul?" Raúl said. "You sing like my eight-year-old daughter."

They all laughed again, and their laughter faded into broad smiles and shaking heads.

"Sorry, I didn't know I was singing out loud." I drove my shovel back into the shimmer, spread asphalt for the steam-roller to crush into the road, hoping they'd let it pass. *Jesus Loves Me*. Not what I wanted.

"No, it's pretty," Raúl said. "Seriously." He drove his shovel down and in spite of myself I noticed his triceps ripple, sweat spraying as he thrust. I hadn't noticed before, his phy-sique, his kindness. His shimmer. This was good because Raúl was sort of a charismatic leader among them, the one to lead a series of crude jokes and also cut them off right before someone got carried away.

"It's good to sing while you work," Salim said. "That's where all them old Negro spirituals came from. Just work." He spat and laughed as if he'd made a joke. It was the most serious thing I'd ever heard him say.

"Jesus loves me this I know," Ken sang.

His voice shocked me, its operatic bass, reminiscent of Paul Robeson. It didn't fit the words.

"Little ones to him belong. They are weak but he is strong."

"Yes, Jesus loves me." They all sang the chorus. "Yes, Jesus loves me. The Bible tells me so."

We sang and shovelled, sang and thrust, and the pain and heat were stapled to our rhythm, part of the song now. I rested my head on the handle of my shovel and inhaled sharply, hoping the sharp stench of asphalt would cauterize my memory.

Sinner. All people have sinned and Jesus died for our sins. I remembered fourteen-year-old Erin in confirmation class, not understanding that. "Like, did he die *because* we sinned, like, we killed him? Or, he died so we could keep sinning? Or was it to *stop* us from sinning?"

I told her something like: all of the above. I was being opaque on purpose, though I'm not sure why. I knew the meaning of the verse, or the way it was interpreted by the church anyway. It just didn't seem to matter.

Erin pursed her neon-pink lips, confused. She was a colourful child. The pink lips, plus green hair, black nails. Always full of questions. I envied her, wished I'd thought of such questions when I was fourteen. Perhaps then I'd have earned a deeper understanding of the wisdom wrapped in a bow and handed to me in seminary. Perhaps then I'd have known what to do with my knowledge.

I tried to imagine my daughter as gangly and awkward and bright and antagonistic as Erin. It was hard to picture her much beyond five years old – I hadn't seen her in that long.

"Think about forgiveness," I said to Erin. I almost asked her to think also about who would be the hardest person for her to forgive. But she was a bright child. It seemed better to leave the matter as wide open as possible.

"Oh," she said, scratching her chin.

Forgiveness. Because all people have sinned, no one has earned the right not to forgive, except perhaps God. "Sometimes we need to pray and ask God's forgiveness," I said.

If only it were that easy. If you are a true believer, to the point that you've lived your life in Christ's love and preached the word for a living, and you can't admit your sins to human beings – not even your wife – how can you admit them to God? Yes, He knows already, but that getting down on your knees and telling Him, that's a physical confrontation with the worst of yourself. It takes supernatural will and strength.

More importantly: I had a particular sin that I was not ready to stop committing.

I went straight home after that confirmation class. That would give me two hours before my family came home.

Sinner.

Love ye poor sinners. Repent.

"Donna, I'm coming in late today. Working on the newsletter."

"Donna, I'm doing a home visit this afternoon. Can't tell you with whom. Very confidential, very sensitive situation."

Computer on. Google: gay sex.

Sinner. Naughty man. Spankings. Rimming. Hand jobs and blow jobs. Hot and wet and loud. Macho men with rippling muscles.

Every site had links to more, more, more sinners, more naughty studs. Shimmering topaz dresses hugging muscular frames: effeminate macho. The perfect turn-on – a gorgeous recent seminary grad seduces a more experienced pastor in a public hot-tub – proved elusive, but quantity was not. Not that I was into younger men. If anything I liked to put myself in a young man's place, imagining myself being guided by an experienced hand. In reality there'd only been Allison and me, two clumsy virgins fumbling in the dark to put tab A into slot B.

In seminary I got by on one Calvin Klein catalogue for four long years. No one ever found it. And if they had found it? "Underwear shopping, duh."

I never regretted becoming a pastor. I believe it was my true calling, a beacon from the darkness of humanity, awash in Christ's blood, pure, non-sexual, my key to the Kingdom when most with my sexual orientation were doomed.

Getting married may have been a mistake. But it gave me Hannah. How can I regret the arrangement that created Hannah? Am I a sinner to say she is my angel, a higher calling than Christ? I carry her picture in my work pants. I show the other men and they show me pictures of their kids. Most of us are separated from them, the product of the unnamed sins of our past. We have all failed as fathers, in one way or another. Raúl ran away; Dave punched his ex; Bunker was addicted to gambling. We envy the ones without kids, without separated hearts. We would sooner go to hell than trade places with them and be childless, an unsaved state of unknown loss.

I regret the Internet. Surely it's the devil's invention. I used to define temptation as George Michael's butt, but what's worse than any sin is its mass distribution. Easy access is the devil's playground.

I was a reluctant user. My secretary signed me up with an e-mail and showed me how to use it. She said it was embarrassing that the priest at Church of the Resurrection, three blocks south of our church, had his own website, where you could download podcasts of his sermons and do a "virtual tour" of the church, and our congregation members couldn't even e-mail me spiritual or logistical questions.

"Move the arrow here with the mouse, right," Donna said, "and click the bottom, the left one, right, and type in hotmail.com – that's h-o-t-m-a-i-l, make sure you put in the right kind of mail, ha ha!"

"What do you mean?"

"Oh, sorry, Reverend, but, you know, just an old joke. You know, you could put in hot *male*, like a sexy man?"

I tugged at my collar.

She smiled.

I cleared my throat and she continued her demonstration.

That night, after Allison and Hannah were asleep, I tried hotmale.com and realized I could get rid of the box in the garage marked "Spiderman Comics: 1970 – 1974." There was even a button that said "clear recent history." Satan's work.

If only I could do that now, delete my history. Delete the three hours I spent "surfing" that night, and the three hours the next night, and the four hours the next morning and the five hours that night, and the forty hours each week after that until I finally got caught in the act six months later when Allison forgot her lunch and came back home for it. "It's not what it looks like," I said. "I'm gay." Whoops – empty bag, say goodbye to cat. So ended both halves of my double life. If my marriage was a sham, so was being a pastor. Being a father wasn't, but I'd lost all credibility with Allison and the church community. So I turned my back on my highest callings – Jesus and Hannah – and I fled.

Even if you somehow deleted that whole pathetic history, you'd still have me. Sinner. Hopeless sinner.

I've watched movies like *Borat* and *Religiosity* and seen the great lengths these guys go to in order to make people feel awkward. It's easier than they know. All you have to do is cry in front of a group of men. And if you can somehow get them to all take their shirts off and do a sing-along child's song first, all the better.

"Oh man, don't cry," Raúl said. "What's wrong, man?" He touched my elbow, a whisper of a caress, as distant as a touch can be. I'd seen Raúl cry once too, when he showed us a picture of his three boys and admitted he left his wife because he knew she stopped loving him the moment their first child was born.

I looked up and saw they had all stopped working, even Bunker, our reluctant crew leader who stuttered and mumbled when he spoke at all, but was the only one born in the same decade I was. He fingered his moustache and stared at me expectantly. They all did.

"Sorry." I sniffed. I was sorry, especially because they had stopped singing. "You're such good singers. Like a choir."

Singers. In the shimmering sun.

"So were those, like, happy tears?" Raúl asked, pulling his hand away and staggering backward like he'd been hit.

"Not exactly."

"C'mon. Let's work," Hector said, scratching at his impressive coat of chest hair.

"Yeah, of course," I said. "I'm sorry." I'd gotten in the habit of apologizing.

We lifted our shovels and struck asphalt in harmony. We stayed in synch for a few more strokes, as if our voices still resonated over the road, still reverberated in the sun. Shimmering sinning singers.

A SPOT OF RED

My first Christmas Eve after my father died I fled to my girlfriend's family, and from there I fled to a graveyard. I don't know for how long I stood staring at the scene before I noticed a little spot of red wedged between two headstones near the back end of the lot. Most of the other headstones were far apart and covered in snow that cascaded like ceramic in a Gaudi sculpture. Bare black trees framed the rear horizon.

My heartbeat steadied looking at it, and I could breathe again, after the perpetual detonation of my girlfriend's mother's apartment, Mags and her brother and sister going at it like split atoms, her mother splayed over the couch launching orders in 360 directions. That was before the aunts and uncles barged in with gifts of moonshine booze for everyone, including Mags' fifteen-year-old sister. I hadn't had a drop, yet there was an axe through my forehead all night, pulsing with the crossed wires of six simultaneous shouting matches. There was no sight nor smell of turkey or fixings. My first Christmas away from home.

A moment came when Don Cherry was yelling from the TV and everyone was yelling back except Mags' mother, who was asleep with her three grown kids sitting on her like she was part of the couch, and Uncle Max raised his glass as if it were a baseball, hooch spilling from it. It was like I'd found a boat outside Alcatraz. I slid on my boots and slipped out the door, no coat or toque. Stupid considering no one had paid me any attention all day. I could have taken the time to prepare for the cold. I panicked, took the chaos with me, and it kept me warm enough, down the hall and three flights of stairs, my legs pumping like I was doing suicides. They kept running over the icy sidewalks of Cove Road all the way to the graveyard.

The apartment, my girlfriend's family conflicts, her siblings' rage, dissolved in my blood, filtered into my lungs, and left my body as visible breath, the fog to complete my northern gothic scene. All that was left in me was an old longing. I missed my father, wished again that he and Mom had me when they were young. He was already old at my birth, and now he was gone. Dead as whatever remained under the frozen headstones. I left Mom alone for her first Christmas without him, thinking I'd found a new family. Mags had described them as wild. I thought she meant that in a fun way.

The little spot of red was still at first, a rose through the ice. Then it moved, and moaned. The sound making its way through the corridor of headstones. It expanded, revealing itself to have limbs, and hands, which pulled at the top of a headstone. It pulled itself up, a man in a red suit. A fat man. Santa Claus.

"Jesus," I said.

"Hello!" he called in response, waving. Disappointingly, no *Ho ho ho*.

"You okay? Santa?"

He gave something of a laugh then, a high whining laugh, like a sharp, long intake of air. "I'm fine."

He took a step forward and fell on his backside, black-booted feet up over his head. I ran to him, sparing a thought for the untouched snow I was inflicting with boot prints. I lifted my feet as high as I could to minimize the damage.

Santa got himself sorted long before I reached him, waving me off and reassuring me. "I'm really fine. I just hit a slippery patch there."

Where his laugh had been off the mark, his voice was marinated in centuries of perfect patience. By the time I reached him I'd convinced myself he had come to this spot to give me a present. Up close I saw the flaws. The belly looked authentic enough but the man wasn't even wearing glasses. His belt had a twelve-inch gold-coloured buckle with the word "Santa" in brush script. Manufactured plastic.

"You come from the mall?"

That wheezing laugh again. "No. Well, I did work this morning but then ..."

I pushed my face toward him, lifting my chin, waiting, but he had lost himself. "Then?"

He shook his head, red cap shifting side to side, a little too big on its perch. The long beard had a patch of grey at the top, making it look real. "Doesn't matter, I'm here now."

"Do you need ... anything? I don't have a car, but I could walk you somewhere."

He nodded and took my arm, linking us at the elbows like an old couple. He looked at me, his face painted with a slack-jawed smile, his teeth nicotine yellow. I took a sniff, searching for that telltale odour of fermentation. No booze, no milk either. Mothballs maybe. We walked to the edge of the grave-yard and down toward the river.

"Big night for you tonight I guess."

"Huh?"

"Where you headed? I'm not from here, but I can come with you." I felt in no hurry to get back to the family kegger. Might be nicer to chat with the old fella. Santa Claus.

"I'm headed to the Oakview Pub," he said. "It's not far."

We spent a while walking along the riverside highway, which funnelled the wind off the frozen river and straight into our faces. We found only car dealerships and churches. One of the latter was open, so we went inside and sat on an empty pew to get warm. Midnight mass would start in a few hours, but at the moment there were only a few clergy shuffling about. One smiled at Santa and gave us a program.

"I hope I can find my way back to my girlfriend's."

"You must be cold the way you're dressed." He leaned his head back, looking in want of a pillow or support, and gave me his open-mouthed smile. I half expected him to invite me to sit on his lap, tell him my Christmas wish. No one could grant me that. When he yawned, I wasn't sure he remembered he was wearing the red suit at all. His breath smelled like tobacco, which reminded me of my father, who was of the generation that thought a dangling lit cigarette looked cool whether you were working under a car, reading a newspaper, or shivering in your galoshes mid-winter because your wife wouldn't let you smoke in the house. The smell took me all the way back to goodnight kisses against scratchy stubble, trying to inhale the strength of him. If this old Santa had put his arm around me in that church and patted my shoulder, I would have found it more comforting than weird. His head was still back, looking up at white arches across the ceiling. It was a town that had invested in its iconography.

"Don't you think you should get back to your girlfriend's? She must be wondering about you."

"I'm wondering about her."

"I see."

"I grew up in a very quiet household." I almost added, *as you know.*

"Only child?"

"Older parents. My girl's mother had her when she was sixteen. I thought that was kind of cool at first, but, I don't know. I think I lost 30 percent of my hearing after one day with them."

"First Christmas away?"

Santa looked exhausted. Was it the 364 days of toy making and letter answering I saw in his yellowed eyes? Hundreds of years of the same routine, same wife and elves and reindeer? Was he longing for something in those white arches above us both? Or was it more the usual, his 9 to 5 at the mall to support ungrateful children demanding the latest gadgetry for

Christmas? My father often complained about my lust for the latest gadgetry. Whether it was a Nintendo Switch or the latest phone, none of it made sense to him the way the sabre saw he got when he was nine did. A gift from Santa, he'd told me.

I slumped down in the pew, thinking about him, and looked up at the old man beside me, around my father's age, his red suit against the vast whiteness of the heavenly ceiling. "I married young," he said.

"Mrs. Claus?"

"Mary Jane Millar. Absolute spitfire. She disowned her own father at our wedding. Caused an insufferable scene. Violently attacked him, accusing him of all kinds of horrible things, most of which were true. She outed him in the most public way possible. For a long time I worried she only married me so she could humiliate her father."

He told a story in much the same way my father had, with a gentle rhythmic lilt and a slight rasp to his voice, in just a few sentences, bold statements with few specifics. He even ended it with a non-conclusive statement.

"Well, why did she marry you?"

He opened his white glove, gesturing to the arches in a twisting motion. "I eventually figured out it didn't matter why she married me. The bigger question was, why did I marry her?"

"Love?"

"She died of alcoholism. That was the cause of her outbursts. I often miss her honesty, but then I'm unsure if that was her or the whisky." He put his arm around me.

I surprised myself with a great sob and apologized.

He pulled me closer, my head against his shoulder.

I became nervous about it and confessed. "You do remind me of my father. He died this year."

"Yep," he said, as if this were common knowledge.

"I probably should get back."

"I should …" He was agreeing with me, but in his uncertain way, reminding me of the time I showed my father how to play Mario Kart. He was into cars, so I thought he'd relate. Dad played three times, finishing last with every effort. He grunted and threw down the controller.

"Do you know where you're going? Santa?"

He looked confused, glancing behind him then patting his bowl-full-of-jelly belly and laughing. "The suit. Forgot I had it on. Yes. I have to go to my daughter's place. On Cove Road."

Outside, he got his bearings and led the way home for both of us, neither of us speaking as we walked. We parted with a handshake at an intersection from where I could see Mags' mom's building. Mags met me at the door to the apartment, frantic and full of questions, kisses, and apologies for the commotion.

I did my best to reassure her. "I just miss Dad is all. Mom too."

She put her arms around my neck and covered my eyelids with cherry lipstick. "Call your mom after we eat."

Inside, her mother was up off the couch, setting the table while a grocery store roast chicken warmed in the microwave. She put down Christmas crackers between the plates, and place names, Mags and me beside one another. When she put out glasses full of red wine, she put the biggest one at my place.

ACKNOWLEDGEMENTS

Some stories in this collection have been previously published:

"Boy With a Problem" in *The Dalhousie Review*, Volume 94, Number 3, 2014

"Operation Niblet" in *Nova Scotia Love Stories*, Pottersfield Press, 2016

"Delia and Phil" in *Earlit Shorts 4*, Rattling Books, 2010

"Home" in *My Nova Scotia Home*, MacIntyre Purcell, 2019

"Realities" in *Galleon IV* December 2015

"Stay Loose" in *The Antigonish Review*, Issue 199, Fall 2019

"Arsonists" in *Fiddlehead*, Number 279, Spring 2019

"Take Him to a Better Place" in *Literally Stories*, October 22, 2019

"Shimmer, Sinner Singer" in *Galleon III*, December 2014

Thank you to the many readers who read earlier, much messier versions of these stories, for their patience and wise council. In particular, thank you to my fellow Wired Monks: Laura Burke, Dina Desveaux, Richard Levangie, Jenni Blackmore, and Simon Vigneault. Thank you, Carole Glasser Langille, Conor McCreery, Randall Perry, Sarah Sawler, and David Huebert, each of whom has read several of these stories, encouraged me, and corrected my course when necessary. And a HUGE thank you Sarah Mian for helping me see what tied these pieces together, and for gifting me with some killer promo copy.

Thank you to all the editors – at publishing houses and literary journals – who worked with me to make these stories as good as they can be, and for accepting them in the first place.

Thank you also to those who turned down my work, especially those who generously offered feedback.

Thank you especially to publisher Lesley Choyce and the team at Pottersfield Press.

Many of these stories were written with the support of the Canada Council for the Arts, in cooperation with the Pictou-Antigonish Regional Library and the South Shore Public Libraries, each of which hosted me as a Writer-in-Residence. Thank you to the many kind staff members who worked hard to welcome and host me, and to the diverse and talented writers who participated in these programs. Please, keep writing!

Lastly, yet most importantly, thank you to my partner and love of my life Miia, who makes all my writing possible in innumerable ways – including being my first and most significant reader.

BOOKS BY CHRIS BENJAMIN

FICTION

Drive-by Saviours

Demoralized by his job and dissatisfied with his life, Mark punches the clock with increasing indifference. He wanted to help people; he'd always believed that as a social worker he would be able to make a difference in people's lives. But after six years of bureaucracy and pushing paper, Mark has lost hope.

All that changes when he meets Bumi, an Indonesian restaurant worker. Moved from his small fishing village and sent to a residential school under the authoritarian Suharto regime, Bumi's radical genius and obsessive-compulsive disorder raise suspicion among his paranoid neighbours. Bumi flees to Canada.

Brought together by a chance encounter on the subway, Mark and Bumi develop a friendship that forces them to confront their pasts. Moving gracefully between Canada and Indonesia and through the two men's histories, *Drive-by Saviours* is the story of desire and connection among lonely people adrift in a crowded world.

NONFICTION

Indian School Road: Legacies of the Shubenacadie Residential School

Journalist Chris Benjamin tackles the controversial and tragic history of the Shubenacadie Indian Residential School, its predecessors, and its lasting effects, giving voice to multiple perspectives for the first time. Benjamin integrates research, interviews, and testimonies to guide readers through the varied experiences of students, principals, and teachers over the school's nearly forty years of operation (1930 to 1967) and beyond. Exposing the raw wounds of Truth and Reconciliation as well as the struggle for an inclusive Mi'kmaw education system, *Indian School Road* is a comprehensive and compassionate narrative history of the school that uneducated hundreds of Indigenous children.

Eco-Innovators: Sustainability in Atlantic Canada

Eco-Innovators profiles some of Atlantic Canada's most innovative and forward-thinking sustainability entrepreneurs, educators, activists, agitators, farmers, and fishers.

In the book, we meet Kim Thompson, a strawbale builder and consultant. Then there's Edwin Theriault, who bought a bale of clothing back in 1971 and launched Frenchy's, a chain of used-clothing stores that has become an East Coast institution. Edwin doesn't consider himself an environmentalist at all, but over the years his business has kept countless tonnes of material out of landfills. Also profiled are Speerville Flour Mill and Olivier Soaps in New Brunswick, Sean Gallagher of Local Source in Halifax, David and Edith Ling of Fair Acre Farm on P.E.I., and Jim Meaney of CanSolAir solar heat air exchangers in Newfoundland, among many others.

With ten chapters on matters like reducing consumption, greening the home, sustainable eating, dressing, transportation, and vacationing, the book is an important look into the lives of Atlantic Canadians committed to creating viable green options in our region. Halifax filmmaker Kevin Moynihan teamed up with Chris to make several short documentaries based on the book (ecoinnovators.org).

ABOUT THE AUTHOR

Chris Benjamin is an author, editor, and freelance journalist specializing in environment, social justice, and arts and culture. He's also a fiction writer.

He earned a marketing communications degree from Dalhousie University. He has since been a market analyst in Waterloo, a forestry officer in St. Lucia, a farm worker in British Columbia, a researcher in Indonesia, a hitchhiker across North America, an advocate for new Canadians in Toronto, a reclusive novelist in Finland, a reluctant train tourist in Russia, Mongolia, China, and Japan, a journalist in Ghana, and an environmental lobbyist in Nova Scotia.

Sometime along the way he picked up a master's degree in Environmental Studies from York University. Chris has been a freelance writer throughout all of his endeavours and has published hundreds of news stories, features, essays, and editorials in various anthologies, newspapers, magazines, and online publications. His fiction has appeared in numerous magazines. He lives in Halifax, Nova Scotia.